VIENNA KISSES
Reflections on a Recipe

❧ ❧ ❧ ❧ ❧

Wilfried G. Lippmann

VIENNA KISSES
Reflections on a Recipe

Wilfried G. Lippmann

Wilfried Lippmann 11-09-06

Mayhaven Publishing

Mayhaven Publishing
PO Box 557
Mahomet, IL 61853

First Edition-First Printing
Copyright © 2003 Wilfried G. Lippmann

Cover Art & Design © Doris R. Wenzel & Aaron M. Porter
LOC: # 2003110197
ISBN: 1878044-93-1
Printed in Canada

❧❧❧ Dedication ❧❧❧

To My Mother

❧ ❧ ❧ ❧ ❧ ❧

Wilfried G. Lippmann also authored the award-winning
book of short stories:

Love Matters
Award-winning Short Stories
Mayhaven Publishing
2001

❧❧❧ Contents ❧❧❧

 1

With a Dough Spoon Forcefully Beaten…

As luck had decreed, Roland Gööck's recipe book and I arrived at the library sale at the same time. The miles and years we had traveled to meet here! We both hailed from Vienna, that famous capital of Austria, thousands of miles away. I was not really attracted to dilapidated books, nor did I have a deep interest in recipe books. What's more, it's paled jacket hung in shreds, barely clinging to the cover. The once bright, mouthwatering photograph on the front remained in bits of jagged images like pieces of a loony puzzle. I could glimpse halves and quarters of golden brown pastries in the shape of pretzels and of half-

9

devoured strawberries on a bed of whipped cream. I opened it up. Some pages were stiff with age, some had become wavy from moisture, some had discolorations. The previous owners had left their marks, their doughy fingerprints, as it were, all over the place. There was not a word of English to be found. One thing was clear. The book dealt with cakes and pastries. The other thing, equally clear, was that the book demanded to be put back. Let another sucker pay the twenty-five cents for this dust-collecting dilapidation.

Yet, my eyes recognized potential pleasures (after all my sweet tooth is as eager for pastry as a dog's canine is for bone). My brain felt challenged to dig around in the pages and bring forth long forgotten German words and sentence structures, and my heart, pumping now at eighty and rising, waxed nostalgic. On the wings of the German words and the fading pastry pictures, I flew back in time when I smelled Mother's baking and heard the smacking of lusty lips in her kitchen. As I thumbed through it, wafts of freshly whipped dough seemed to rise into my nostrils. I was a kid again, waiting for Mother to let me into the kitchen to lick the dough spoons clean.

I paid my twenty-five cents and Roland's work was mine. Its title was *Backen mit Lust und Liebe*"—Bake with

Lust and Love. But German lust is not what it purports to be. We're talking joy here, perhaps even anticipated joy. Be that as it may, lust bubbles up, after all, from intense anticipated joy, namely to devour baked delicacies. So, to stifle the harsh German and soften the image, why not keep the lust out of the act of baking and lay all blame on the lusty pastries themselves, those instruments of persuasion, of lecherousness, lasciviousness, and promiscuity, those insidious conquerors and purveyors of otherworldly palatine sensibilities?

As I stopped to read a paragraph here and an explanation there, I shook my head in disbelief. Did I really speak this language once? Isn't a.German supposed to be a rather straightforward, geometric, one-two-three figure whose language you'd expect to match his demeanor? As evidence I offer a sentence from page 45 out of Gööck's book, a recipe book, mind you, whose sole intent should be to be precise and clear, and brief.

Let the dough mass, which by the flour indented and with one teaspoon sugar on yeast filled was created and in lukewarm milk and a little flour to a pre-dough formed and for 20 to 30 minutes covered risen, then with milk, flour, butter, sugar, lemon rind, salt and eggs to a smooth consistency with a dough spoon forcefully beaten and stirred and kneaded, finally with overheated and in flour tumbled raisins and chopped candied lemon nd ground walnuts into it diligently incorporated, covered for another for 20 to thirty minutes and then heartily worked over, into a greased pan flow and after 15 to 20 minutes bake.

Clear as mud. Easy as $E=mc^2$.

ぉぉぉ 2 ぉぉぉ

Of rum, of chocolate, of addiction, and a fine corpse...

Roland's book looked abused, but the streaks of dried dough and the colorful spots on its pages told me tales of busy kitchens in the turmoil of a family baking event. I found a chocolaty index fingerprint, a child's surely, on a description of a chocolate-nut-biscuit roll laden with strawberries. Did that naughty boy get his dough dipping fingers smacked with the stinging metal of a beater? Oh, yes. "There will be no cake for you, little thief," his mother had surely cried. But of course there was. The thief was forgiven, the tears dried, kisses were given all around.

I imagined the widow Kowalski, from the old neighborhood in Vienna, could have, on page 37, crossed out the 2 of "2 El (= 2 Tsp) of rum" and written the big red 4? Rum lover Kowalski spiked her Marmorkuchen, to the delight of her Kaffeeklatsch ladies who praised the delectable cocoa marbling openly, "Oh, the cocoa marbling is so perfect," I hear them say, "How do you get it just so?" But it was the rum, really, the sweet-toothed liars were after.

The widow, left behind by the dead Major Kowalski, was still young at forty-two, childless and with a certain post-war eagerness, knew of the power of baking. I do recall a circumstance. The rum went well with the ladies, but an exquisite serving of virgin white meringue shells with vanilla ice cream topped with sculpted whipping cream and tart liquor-soaked cherries (if one could get hold of them), now that was what a man could get addicted to— a man like the undertaker, Franz Riedl—*her* undertaker Franz Riedl. This director of the beloved departed, who had buried the Major and made the arrangements to produce class "a fine corpse" as he simply called it, complete with seraphic bells and an Ava Marie, the same Riedl who had IOU's from hundreds of bereaved women for whom he had officiated free of charge at their husband's "corpses", this calculating burier of the earthly leftovers came to call on the post-war merry widow Kowalski often and cashed in a small chit by delectating in her generous meringue offering.

"How's my favorite merry widow?" began Franz Riedl as she opened her door. To him all widows were merry, or soon would be. She invited him in and he hung his hat and walking stick on the hallway hook and sat down in the same chair on the same side of the same table as he did on the day of the Major's fine corpse. His right arm shot straight forward to clear his wrist from his cuff, then he bent the elbow and cupped his ear. In short order he was lapping from the spoon, the remnants of the married widow's classy dessert. Could the attractive widow Kowalski have sunk so low as to cater to Herr Riedl of the Central Cemetery for anything else but to thank him for the free "corpse" of the Major? She could. Let us not forget that life was lonely for the millions of widows after the war for whom there were not enough men left to go around. And let us not arrogantly dismiss their need to be wanted for any reason whatsoever.

I conjure for you Frau Kunkel, the voluminous half of the caretaker couple of building four on the Liechtensteiner Street, who, I suspect, caused the discoloration and wrinkles, which I had observed when I first fingered the book, in the chocolate section. We have to understand that Wilhelmine

Kunkel was an addict. The years of her addiction had made her round, solidly round, chocolate round. She had become so round that the slender Herr Kunkel looked like an insignificant sliver of a man next to her. Worse, he could no longer satisfy his romantic needs. "Finished" he had cried one day, at the end of his rope, "Wilhelmine, we are finished. No more chocolate! We can not do anymore—we can not—" The poor man's voice faltered.

"Oh, my little broomstick," said Wilhelmine with sorrow in her eyes. "I can not help it. It's the chocolate." She resolved to lay off the chocolate, again. She would fail. When Johann was out to fix the elevator or clean the courtyard, out came the baking bowls, the stirring and whirring devices, the ingredients, the chocolate, and Roland Gööck. But Johann had caught on. He wasn't going to be swept aside any longer with "my little broomstick." He tiptoed up to her from behind. Wilhelmine's breath was heavy, her face aglow. Her heart pumped to the rhythm of her beaters, her eyes rested lovingly on the creaming mass of pure sin in her bowl.

"Aha!" Herr Kunkel suddenly hollered at the top of his lungs. "Inflagranti!"

The startled woman flung the chocolate bowl into the

air, the beaters dropped and bounced, flinging rich brown dough into every direction. Her hands clasped her heart. The good Frau Kunkel, like her bowl, had also keeled over, and Roland Gööck's book was forever marked.

The multi-colored blotch on pages 320 and 321 looked like the imprint of the shortbread tart with almonds and marmalade whose recipe was on the same page. Someone heavy had inadvertently sat down on the book and just as inadvertently had press a tart flat like a leaf in a plant collection between the two pages. That someone was, of course, the fat Hans who was cookie crazy and whose mother rewarded him with a double ration if only he'd be a good boy, and even if he wasn't comma, just to shut him up.

As I reflected on the many hands and fingers that had walked through the pages, my thumb hesitated on page 227, an odd clear page—in the chocolate section of Kunkel fame. It was the home page for Vienna Kisses. No egg splatter, no nut fragment had found its way onto this page to obscure the words. Strong memories flooded my senses. I could smell the hearty hazelnuts, the unsettling odor of chocolate, and the coffee granules ground to powder, that the recipe demanded. I heard the grating noises, the slop and slosh of the moist dough mass. I breathed it all in. I took an imaginary bite of a kiss and rolled it around in my mouth like a wine connoisseur swirls a sip of the precious liquid. Like a real kiss on the lips, the initial rough texture softened and melted away into the tongue, the gums, the throat.

The memories had me by the scruff. Right there, still in the library where I had sunk into one of the scattered reading chairs, I nearly called out to Mother to beg just one more before bed. Please! And I heard my sister Rose clamoring angrily—and successfully, "If angel-face there," she said, and threw me a withering glance, "if *he* can have one, so should I!"

Roland Gööck's Recipe
Vienna Kisses

Ingredients
3 Eggs
200 grams powdered sugar
1 tsp vanilla extract
350 grams finely grated hazelnuts
1 tsp of coffee, ground into powder
50 grams finely grated baking chocolate
1-2 tsp of rum extract
marmalade or cherry jam

Step 1
Separate three egg whites from the yolks,
Beat the egg whites until stiff with solid peaks...

❧❧❧ 3 ❧❧❧

Carry three eggs carefully in your bra...

Rose was a force of one. She was only two years older than I but her motto was survival of the poking forefinger, especially as it related to that dumb, unfairly cute brother—*me*. I felt that forefinger in my ribs before it actually hit. And I knew it was coming when mother made a certain racket in the kitchen. Her bang-slam oom-pa-pa of pots and pans when she was cooking became tempered with the soft brushing sound and the glob-cluck-slap of a spoon or a hook thickening the dough when she was baking. That was sweet music to us and it drew us irresistibly. Rose made me hide behind the doorpost and peek out. "What's Mother doing now?" she hissed in my ear standing behind me. Then she poked and poked and poked. "Now smile your angelic stupid smile," she ordered and poked. Oh, that forefinger! But there, only a few feet away stood my wonderful mother with her back to us in full baking regalia. She was clad only in blouse and bloomers—she had removed her skirt to find relief from the heat of oven and exercise—and her apron. She hummed and tra-la-la-ed in perfect rhythm to the shaking of her ample behind, golden locks and clacking beaters.

Finally, when Mother had whipped this and stirred that and when she finally interrupted her happy baking dance, the long awaited words came forth from her lips. "What is that?" she asked with mock surprise. "I heard something. It couldn't be Rose and Willy, could it?" Then we stormed forth from behind the door, screaming, "yeah, yeah, it's us, it's us!" Rose was first, of course—she had clamped her strong fist on my forearm and pushed herself forward and me backward. But we hung on Mother's legs and arms like children dying of hunger and thirst, pleading for—for—well for something out of the baking pan. Rose got what I got, and I got what Rose got. Mother never played favorites when it came to offering us beaters to lick (there were always two), a bowl to finger-clean (there were always two bowls—miraculously), a stray handful of nuts to share (there was always an even number of nuts—equally miraculous). I like to think that my sweet smile did it all and Rose should have thanked me. Of course, she didn't. Such is life with an older sister. What would she have done without me?

Cookies or anything else resembling sweets baking in a hot oven had become rare in the months before the end of the war. Now, after its end, prospects for such homey events were getting worse before they got better. Our childish hopes that the end of the war would quickly restore everything as it had been were dashed when the whole city, as we knew it, had ceased to exist. But miracles were possible, nevertheless. In our young minds we imagined an uprising of millions of bricks to make walls again, and buildings as they had been; bomb fragments made whole bombs again and then they flew up from the ground to reunite with their airplanes whence they had come; burned out trams and their twisted, drooping electric guide wires suddenly untangled and restored themselves; gaping craters filled in to become smooth streets again. Our hopes for those sweet kisses hot out of the oven could not be denied. They hung around our eyes and Mother saw them every day. "Someday again," she told us. We had to be patient and be glad we had some things to eat. Period. "Look at yourselves," she said sadly and touched my flat cheeks and Rose's dangling arms, skinny as long noodles and knobby as bare ash branches in winter. Everything was rationed. How could there be extra eggs for baking? Let alone nuts, vanilla, chocolate?

It wasn't long before Mother took drastic steps to increase our food supply. Rationed goods went only so far. But to feed an eight-year-old body going on nine, and a girl's ten-year-old one, nearing eleven, growing out of control so it seemed, required more than the piddling amount from the ration card. There never were enough potatoes, vegetables, eggs. Eggs. Where to get eggs? They said that not enough hens had survived the hunger period in late '44 and early '45. Then the Russians had swamped the farming areas to the east and potatoes and eggs were under the strictest control. First they fed themselves, then they let the farmers have a bit to keep on working. Whatever was left came into the city.

"The weak link," my mother told Frau Tomes, a neighborhood friend, one morning when they met at the food depot, "It is the farmer. They hoard. Of course they hoard. That's where we must go. Directly to the source."

"Now yes, but—" doubted Frau Tomes and she laughed nervously.

"You can say as many buts as you like. You have a daughter, no? Do you want Karin to be a healthy girl? Look at her. She looks hollow cheeked like my Willy. He's also eight."

"What do you have in mind? You know I'm not brave."

Frau Tomes could already figure out what my mother had in mind. They knew each other well. They had met in '43 in the air-raid shelter. Frau Tomes had cried and Mother had prayed.

"Crying isn't going to help us any," Mother had said.

Frau Tomes wiped the dripping off her pointed nose. "No, I think not, of course. But what has praying done to keep the bombs away?"

"One must have belief, my dear," Mother said gently. "The army will come through."

Of course the army did *not* come through. It was the beam of light that people were told to hang on to for deliverance. Have faith, had been announced at every street corner. The setback would only be temporary.

"We go. If you don't want to come, I go alone," Mother said with finality. "Friday. Off at nine at night. It'll be dark. Wear dark clothes. Well?" Mother's voice was strong, matter of fact, but she was trembling inside. I had seen her say strong words and then later she had cried quietly in a dark corner. She secretly hoped that the diminutive Anna Tomes found the guts to come along. Two is always better than one.

Frau Tomes stammered. She wanted to and then she didn't want to.

She needed food, yes, she fretted silently. Ration cards just didn't cut it. "What do they think we are? Hunger artists? There could be potatoes, carrots, cabbage, turnips. My little Karin needs it all. Quietly crawl through the field and take them out. Simple. But what about eggs? We couldn't just go into the hen house and steal the eggs. What a ruckus! We'd be caught. Killed maybe. Then where would we be? Everybody knows what happened in Kalksburg and the Naschmarkt, my God they shoot looters and thieves, don't they? Then there was the danger with the Russians. If it hadn't been for the officers of the second wave…they had warned us of the Third Ukrainians. What if they stopped us, even now after the end of the shooting and bombing? What to do, what to say—my God."

"Yes. Karin. She'll benefit, certainly—now yes, then," she finally stammered in agreement. She had made a decision. It was good to have made a decision. One can gain energy and the spirit rises. Most of all, one is not alone. She bubbled over. "The Frau Major might come along too. She's a sturdy woman. Polish stock. Surely she'll help us. She can carry more than we can. You know her? You've seen her?"

Mother was glad. Now they were three. Three is better than two. "What could they do to us three if they caught us? Nothing, surely. This is good. We can support each other." The last time she went to steal she did it alone, back in March, only weeks before the end. Then she saw it happening right in front of the department store, all the people silently staring. This she will never forget. They stood the poor man up at the edge of the crater—pistol to the back of the head—boom. Shot him dead—just like that. "He was a thief," the executioners told the crowd. How the thief crumbled into the crater. Gone. What had he stolen from the grand Kaufhaus? Something for his wife, something for his son or daughter, maybe some flour and salt from the warehouse next door? She had taken off at a fast pace, looking back over her shoulder at every corner, but she had held on to her bags. Warm shoes for Rose and Willy. Shawls for the

cold weather. Maybe the
worn clothes of an ordina.
derer himself and a deserter. l\
all around. Ah, kill him if you like. s.
children. What mattered more than they
were three. Yes, three was much better. When they
we'll do a bit of yelling, then crying, then maybe mak\
eyes to the men. We all know what they want. Then they'll
let us off and we'll get back. We have to get back. The children, they would be waiting.

They were widows. All three had learned to take charge
of their lives without the men. Necessity bred creativity.
Necessity created energy. Three women in the prime of their
lives, two with children in tow. The Frau Major had no children but a nephew and a niece somewhere in the vast dev-
astated city. Children can't grow on ration cards. As an
adult, one can survive. It takes a harsher life than this to die.

They all had saved their cigarette allotments. Good bargaining chips.

"Make sure to bring your cigarettes," Mother told them.
"They are as good a bribe as any."

"Not as good as your body. Nobody dies," said Frau
Tomes with a sheepish grin.

hat are you saying? Just because it happened when
Ukrainians first swept into the city, they were all unedu-
ted peasants, you know—the war is over. At any rate,
screaming is best. The officers will come right away. Did
you not scream at the top of your lungs? Did they not spray
the house with the Russian letters 'k n', you know, for block
checked, so we'd be safe?"

"Yes, yes," Frau Tomes admitted. But she knew as
everybody else knew that the body was the best bargaining
chip of all when a life, especially a child's life, were at
stake.

"Bring cigarettes," Mother insisted.

The electric streetcar to the farming district Floridsdorf
had been opened just weeks after the war's final grenade.
Mountains of rubble had been moved off the tracks and
piled high left and right. The ride was rough. Cracked tracks
shook the creaky conveyance. It could collapse at any
moment. Yet, the driver let it run. He had tempted fate all
war long and survived. This tram run was a piece of cake.
No one complained about anything. Not the wind blowing
through the smashed windows, not the splintered seats

whose wooden parts had been appropriated last winter. One stood in the tram inwardly thinking, inwardly planning, and pulling the flimsy clothes around one's skinny body. But now the warm weather was approaching. Life looked better. One could converse, although it was mostly about survival, food shortages, illnesses, the treatment of soldiers. But energy was projected outward. The tram ran. One could get the ration cards at the central authority downtown in the first district just off the Ringstraße. Better than walking over the mountainous landscape of brick and chunks of concrete embedded in dust.

They wore dark dresses that looked like sacks and the sturdiest shoes they could muster. Potato sacks hid under their skirts. They had stuffed cigarettes into their socks. Dark scarves covered Mother and the Kowalski woman. They were both blond.

"Beauties we are not," said the Frau Major. "They'll let us go simply on that count." She grinned with thin, pale lips. Her blue eyes were tired, her eyebrows too bushy. Her body was slim yet sturdy, judging from her stride and ample bosom—the opposite of Tomes who seemed to have no bosom. The little woman wore an ankle length skirt that swirled around her feet threatening to entangle her. Her face was drawn taut, her nose protruding even more than usual. She held her fists tight around herself.

"You are tense. And why did you wear such a long skirt? What if we had to run?" demanded Mother.

"I hold it up, like that," Frau Tomes said and grabbed her hem and pulled it exposing her bare white legs and the potato sack dangling between them.

"All right. Relax. We are after food and we are going to get it. Here comes the tram."

The tram screeched, throwing sparks from the iron wheels. In the twilight, the tram looked like a torn vehicle from hell, bearing down on them along the rubble-engulfed street.

"Where to, my ladies?" called the driver. "I'll lead you to the edge of Russia. Comrade Stalin's friends are waiting for you, what?" He grinned.

"Hold your smart mouth. Nothing of the kind," Mother told him harshly, faking deep upset. "We are visiting sick people, get it? Sick people. Would you leave your mother or friend without any help at all?"

"Come now, come now," laughed the driver, stubbles on

his chin and a tram driver cap without any insignia whatever. "You can tell me. It's my last trip to Floridsdorf today. You won't be riding with me tonight again."

"You couldn't wait for us, could you?" tried Frau Tomes. "We'd have to walk back all this way."

"Crazy women," he said quietly. He knew full well what was what. He had a mind to join them. "I just can't. I won't jeopardize my job. My extra ration card is at stake here."

As though he wanted to put emphasis on his excuse he sped on with especially loud rattling and screeching in the dangerous curves. Darkness descended. The tram's headlight weakly lit the metal rails ahead.

"I let you off here. See these woods to the right? They were spared from the axe-men. A miracle after last winter, what? They practically ruined the Wienerwald already." The tram came to a halt. "Step through the woods quietly, listen for the Russian gibberish. They use the woods for cigarette breaks and to relieve themselves. On the other side is a narrow valley, cross it and the fields begin. Keep low. The farmers are known to keep an eye out for people like you coming from the city to steal. I've heard it all. Off you go, now. Maybe I'll see you again, maybe I won't. Off!" He was saying his final "off" roughly, like an unwilling order.

31

"We're just seeing our sick relatives." Frau Tomes said with a drawn smile that exaggerated her nose.

"Yeah, yeah. Off, I said." He looked at them descending the rickety steps. Marvelous women, he thought. I wish them luck. He shook his head and pushed the tram lever forward. The tram lurched like an old man on his deathbed. It rattled fearfully. Would it last another run?

The three women headed east into the unknown. Another detail had come from the tram driver, an invaluable piece of information to help them along. Mother had picked up bits and pieces of conversations flying around in shop lines and on the brick removal details earning extra ration cards. Floridsdorf had always been a reliable farming district. The fertile inundation plane of the Danube was ideal for the growth of fresh foods that the city needed. Now the district lay firmly in the hands of the Russians. The way she saw it, safety lay in avoiding the Russian patrols, avoiding the farmer. Her heart beat a little heavier than before. But she had to remain strong. The other two counted on her. But what really mattered were Rose and Willy. We both had stared at her, as if we knew of the danger she was putting herself in, with large saucer eyes—so large because her orders were so harsh—we both had stared at her in silent fear.

"Let's move," she said gruffly. "This way. And quiet. You heard the tram driver."

No one had a compass. No one had any training in orientation. Whether the moon was to the left or right, or straight overhead, it meant little. A bit of light from it helped distinguish between the dark shapes of trees and those of buildings. The rest was a matter of feeling the earth through the soles of their shoes, of smelling field or trees, of hearing the rustling of leaves and the calls of toads and crickets. Necessity pushed them on. Completeness of this mission was the motive. Food was the reward.

They had heard nothing unusual as they traipsed through the forest. The open field would be just beyond. The dense wood suddenly opened up. As if the moon had freed itself from the wispy clouds on their behalf, it shone a pale light onto the quiet landscape ahead. Just as the tram driver had said, orderly rows extended into the distance. The shadowy potato plants told them of the treasures that lay beneath them in the rich earth. The women fell to their hands immediately. They reached under their skirts for the bags. Side by side, they scooted forward on their knees, oblivious to the damp earth, not minding scrapes on hands or dirt on their dress.

The work was easy. The spuds dropped into the sacks, one by one. The deep fullness of the earth filled their noses and clung to their bare hands as they scraped clumps of dirt from the life-giving food. They could not contain themselves. At first they whispered, then they talked in almost normal tones. Everything was so easy they felt as though they were on a sanctioned outing. It was wonderful. The potatoes were firm. They would make them last. One must help oneself, one can not wait for the provisionary government to hand it to them. The children were growing, they had been deprived of so much. Look at their undernourished bodies. It was easy to leap forward in time and already smell the sizzling Bratkartoffel and hear the children shout in delight.

"Quiet," called the Frau Major suddenly. As if on cue the three women stretched full length into the ditch between the rows. They buried their white faces in their scarves and their hands underneath their bodies. Their ears were singularly tuned for the faintest noise. A male voice from far off drifted to them. The words were unintelligible, but they were followed by a door opening and then falling shut, and by a subdued rustle of animal feathers.

"It's only the farmer," said Mother, "checking on the chicken house."

"We are about done here. Let's go back to the tram tracks before he catches us." Frau Tomes had had enough.

"Nonsense," insisted Mother. "When he leaves the chicken house we'll go in and get some eggs."

"You are crazy," said Kowalski, laughing. "You can never get enough."

"We will leave our full sacks here. We gather the eggs in the scarves, then—"

"There he is already."

The farmer had left the chicken house and headed back to his house. The door slammed.

"Now, come!" Mother commanded.

The noise in the chicken house was deafening. It seemed the chickens protested at the top of their voices. They knew instinctively that nothing good would come of the presence of the three witches of the night. The women with dirty dresses, smeared faces and hands, wild unkempt hair, head scarves in their hands, rushed through the coop grabbing eggs left and right, scattering chattering hens in all directions. It was the extra egg that each woman wanted to gather up that did them in.

"Halt!" roared the farmer, standing in the door frame. "What are you doing? Who are you? Stealing, you are stealing. You are stealing my eggs! What if everybody comes here to steal eggs? But I have you now. You will not escape. They shoot thieves and looters, you know. Don't you know that?" He was beside himself. He nearly jumped up and down and pounded one fist into the other at this outrage.

"Yes, we know that," retorted Mother defending them all. "But why do we have to do this? We have children to feed. There's not enough food—"

"Don't give me the cry story. Thieves you are. Thieves. Show me your identification cards."

"Don't be such an authority. We don't bring identification. Do you think we are crazy?"

"Please don't turn us in. We will never come back," whined Frau Tomes. "Here. Here. Take back the eggs. All of them."

"Yes, I want all of them back," said Farmer Oh-so-tough. But his voice was milder. He had reacted to the little Tomes, who appeared as small as a child herself. "And if I ever see you again, I will turn you in. Verstehen Sie das?"

So the three women turned around and gave back the eggs to the squawking hens while the farmer raved on about his hard work and stealing riffraff, and the demanding Russian soldiers that didn't leave him barely enough to feed his own family.

But Mother was not so easily rebuffed. She elbowed Kowalski and showed her in one instant how to shove some eggs into her bra. While talking soothingly to the protesting hens, both Mother and Frau Kowalski had secured four eggs in the warm, soft cleavage between their breasts. Frau Tomes, who was not amply endowed, barely managed to squeeze two into her garment.

Showing the farmer their empty scarves and tying them again to their heads, they walked out. They appeared to be crying. But it was the pungency of the surroundings that made their eyes water. No matter. The farmer only mumbled something and looked away. Crying mothers were not his favorite adversaries.

"What has the world come to. Pure survival. Oh good God," he mumbled in lieu of a farewell and shook his head.

The women reached their potato sacks and flung them over their shoulders. It was time to head home.

"We've even saved our cigarettes." Mother smiled at this good fortune.

At the edge of the woods they rested. The sacks were

Wilfried G. Lippmann

heavy. The walk home would be long and arduous.

"No, no," cried Frau Tomes suddenly. "I've crushed my eggs. Eek. It's running down my skin. Eek."

"Cry not so loud, for the will of God," said Mother. But it was already too late. Three gun muzzles suddenly appeared out of nowhere and pointed directly at their faces.

"Shto?" yelled the tall soldier. His eyes were drawn close together. His Kalakhnikov nearly touched the nose of Frau Tomes. "Shto?"

Frau Tomes, feeling her crushed egg slide into the nether regions of her body held her arms around her stomach to hold up the cold yellow mess. "I don't speak Russian," she wailed. "No one does."

"We go home. We have potatoes. You want them? Here—" Kowalski opened her bag of potatoes.

But the Russians weren't from yesterday. They knew damned well what was in the sacks. They may even have watched them the whole time and had laughed their heads off when the farmer caught them red-handed. They looked the women up and down. Finally, their rifles pointed down. Mother thought the danger was over.

"It is for the children, little children," she said, pointing down to her knee level to mark their heights. "What is the

38

word in Russki, I forget, little children, ah, deeati. Deeati! At home!"

"Deeati?" said the man in front of her. He was a small man with a Stalin mustache and he smelled earthy and was spitting out bits of turnip. Then he turned to his fellow mates and said deeati. The other repeated deeati. The third, his cap like an upturned rowboat sitting askew and tilting dangerously over his right ear, said deeati. Then they roared with laughter.

The women didn't know what to think. First the guns in their faces and then merry laughter. But suddenly the men became serious. They pointed at each one, argued "mayah" (mine) and "mayah" and "mayah," changed places, then closed in. The guns dropped to the ground. In seconds the women had been pushed roughly to the ground over their desperate objections. None of the woman was naïve to think what was about to happen wouldn't happen. They also knew that screaming wouldn't help, not here in no-man's-land. Should they plead? It was too late. All they could do was mumble their prayerful no's.

The soldiers, quick and agile, battle and post-battle experienced, had themselves unbuttoned, the women pinned and made vulnerable in a second.

"Think of your life," the women said to themselves. They turned their faces to each other with wet and pained eyes. "Think of your child. Think of tomorrow."

The men groaned and stood as quickly as they had come down. It was all over.

"Davai!" they yelled waving their guns in the direction of the woods. "Davai!" The cold steel of the gun muzzles poked harshly against their arms. The women scrambled to their feet, grabbed their sacks and stumbled into the darkness of the woods. There was no stopping them until they had reached the other side where the empty tram tracks greeted them in the pale moon.

"We've made it," said Frau Tomes through tears that dripped off the tip of her nose.

The women fell into each other's arms.

"Let's go home, quick" said Mother. "The children are waiting."

"Hear me," said the Frau Major. "Wash yourselves hard when you get home." The good practical Frau Major Kowalski. She was going to use alcohol. She had some stored, even if it was only rum.

They parted where they started. They were dead tired. All they had thought about was to make it back home. They had not been thinking of their haul. They had forgotten the eggs. Until now.

"The eggs, the eggs," said Kowalski. "How did the eggs fare?"

"I have one intact," Tomes piped up.

"All four. It's a miracle," said Mother, tears in her eyes. "After what we've been through—"

"Me too," confirmed Kowalski, and she reached into her brassiere. Between thumb and forefinger appeared the perfect egg, gleaming so white and virtuous. "Here," she said to Tomes.

"Here," said Mother and gave her one of hers. "Equal rewards for equal pains. You could use a little more padding, you know, Anna Tomes."

Roland Gööck's Recipe
Vienna Kisses

Step 2
Combine egg whites with powdered sugar and vanilla
extract and mix until smooth…

4

Did I bring something sweet? I brought myself, Sugar.

When eggs were in the house, the prospects for Vienna Kisses rose dramatically. But Mother found herself short of sugar and nuts and one of the other ingredients. So, it meant waiting. When would we hear the spoons and whisks and beaters clack and whir? When would we be able to admire the hard beaten egg whites that looked like the ragged Alps? And when, in a dish off to the side, would we see the three lonely yolks shimmering golden and looking at us like the three eyes of a kind ogre? Would they not turn into Sunday morning egg crepes, smeared with jam and rolled and sprinkled with powdered sugar, by Mother's magic hands? Aaaah.

When we stuck our forks into food we had to eat and images of Vienna Kisses danced in our heads, we found it hard to clean the plates. In the months following the war it was unwise to throw something away. Criminally unthrifty. An outgrown shirt could bring a pair of mittens, a pair of shoes could bring two packs of cigarettes which could buy a loaf of bread. Potholders were made from winter socks. But to leave food on the plate, let alone refuse to eat it, my God, that was a sin, if not a sin an affront, if not an affront an accusation.

"It seems you are too well off," Mother would abruptly turn her wrath on us when we shook our heads at the awful looking meal. "You have too much, what? Now then, I had planned on some sweets," she lied wagging her finger, "but I'll have to cut that out, so it seems. We just have to make you a little bit hungrier first."

When we heard that, we knew she was lying, but just on the outside chance that she was going to bake something, we lapped up the rest like starving dogs, praying to God to make it come true.

"Now this is more like normal behavior," she'd say then, mollified.

One day, out of the blue, Aunt Leni and Jutte, her teenaged daughter, stood in front of our door with their meager belongings.

Our story and Aunt Leni's story were simple war stories of suddenly desperate and homeless people. Women with children were the victims. Their own apartments had been bombed into heaps of rubble. They squatted in someone's abandoned flat if they could find one. It was a dark wish that the true owners had been killed or taken away to Siberia. The housing authority was slow in acquiring the long arms needed to reach and help the shelterless on the street. At first, there was a daily appeal that traveled by word of mouth, later by radio, and still later by newspaper. Don't turn down the homeless, the appeal said, even if they are already occupying your former apartment—which they would surely leave as soon as other shelters could be found or built. But the appeals fell on deaf ears. In the early days after the war survivalist self interest prevailed. "Protect yourself." "Keep the riffraff away." "It's hard enough alone." Those were the thoughts that slammed doors into many a face. Lucky were the ones squatting unmolested in someone else's apartment, lucky were the ones finding shelter in one of the cavernous anti-aircraft towers, lucky were the ones finding kind folks willing to take one or two into their cramped quarters. Lucky were the ones finding relatives with whom they could stay.

We were among the lucky ones. Mother had had a determined eye. Door-to-door, house-to-house, block-by-block, district-by-district she dragged us, from one old friend's remembered place to another. Dead tired, we climbed heaps of rubble only to find another prospect had ended up no better than what had happened to our own place, which had disintegrated with the rest of the apartments into a mountain of brick, concrete and rebar. We spent the nights huddled under a concrete overhang or in a hollow in the side of a brick mountain, Rose warming her knobby frame on Mother's left, and I snuggling close to her right. As long as we had Mother's soft warmth protecting us we were confident that something soon would turn up. If Mother ever cried, she sure hid it well.

But we were lucky. It took only a chance glance. A reflection off a piece of glass had caught Rose's eye.

"Mother," she had cried out, "look at the stairwell. It goes clear to the top."

Mother did not hesitate to assess the situation as a potential find. A path wound itself around piles of brick and other debris and it led to the stairwell. We closed in, tender footed like weary discoverers in a brick jungle. We had to look out for precarious overhangs, razor-edged blocks of concrete and twisted rebar that could poke us in the eye or slash us across the face. Rose's stairwell turned out to be solid. It spiraled up from landing to landing, ascending in right angle loops around a wire cage center space reserved for the elevator. We couldn't see the elevator itself but the cable seemed solid and taut, reaching up beyond the fifth floor and vanishing into the dark roof section. We finally spied the dusty wooden box resting at the lowest level, the cellar. It was the elevator that would bring to our door, once electricity was restored, the young and dashing Martin from the Alsergrund Military Jail.

"People already live here," said Mother. I couldn't see anyone, but at each landing there was a door to the right and one to the left. It seemed the doors to the right were in better condition. They were cleaner. They had a shield attached giving a name, and they were locked. The left doors hung crooked on their hinges, slightly ajar. Through the cracks we saw what lay beyond—nothing. That part of the great apartment building had been ripped away by a bomb.

"Stay here, guard the suitcases," Mother had said to us.

"I'll ask around."

As I said, we were one of the lucky ones. The top floor, Mother was told, was not occupied. So, we moved in.

We were looked at with suspicion. Children were nowhere in sight. Was this a building full of child enemies? When Rose and I ran up and down the stairwell taking two steps at a time, sometimes even jumping from four steps up to the landing, the whole stairwell seemed to shake and vibrate. A door would open on floor four and the shriveled childless Schuster sisters would stick out their long beaked noses and their crooked fingers would wave at us. Then, in a cackling voice, they admonished us that this was not a playground and that people need quiet and rest. "OK, sorry," we called out cheerfully, and in a whispering giggle added, "you old goats." Mother always called them that when they complained about this or that triviality.

On floor three lived the Kravitzes, an old couple, who stayed to themselves. I only saw them once. They were so old and black and bent that they reminded me of the witch in *Hänsel and Gretel*. But they never looked at us. We thought they weren't even aware we existed. Surely, they were no longer solid in the brain. "It's a sad thing," Mother said. "They've come through two wars and now all they can do is wait for death to come for them, which they had so gallantly avoided." Rose and I couldn't see anything gallant in these old people with walking sticks.

On floor two lived the Backuses. But there were no kids. The only time they had a child there was when some- one visited. And then they stayed indoors most of the time. One time we coaxed the little girl, her name was Mariechen, to come out and play with us. We took her clear to the base- ment and showed her the coal cellar and the collapsed brick wall to the storage area. If we were quiet enough and stood there watching we could see the rats scurrying around. At the sight of the fat marauding rats she let out a primeval scream and ran back upstairs where, instead of comfort, she found a threatening hand and a bitter scolding, "Marieeeeechen! Damn you!" As she tried to take the steps two at a time she bunched up her dress to climb better and I could see that she didn't have any underpants on. The Backus folks, Mother told us, were refugees from the east and one couldn't trust them until one got to know them bet- ter. But there was no chance for that. They were out before we passed their door in the morning and back in when we came home from school and play.

On floor one lived a single woman, Regina Klahn, who

claimed that her mother, aunt and uncle and their children would soon arrive and live with her. But Mother had her figured out really quick. She didn't want anyone to live with her. "She is one of those," Mother explained.

"One of what those?" I asked.

"Why must you know everything, what?" But my sister knew. "Men," she whispered in my ear and poked hard with her forefinger. "Men are coming in and out." So what, I thought. Who cares?

On the Mezzanine floor lived the Schwartzes, a grumpy couple. She was the only fat person I had ever seen. Herr Schwartz was short and grouchy at all times of the day, especially when he saw me and Rose. We were kids and that meant trouble somewhere along his path. They were the Hausmeisters, responsible for the orderly conduct of all people living in this building. Everyone who lived there was registered with them. They maintained the stairs and the elevator after it had been repaired. They locked the great, newly hung street-side door every night. After it got dark everyone was supposed to be in the house. If one was late, Herr Schwartz with the big key had to be called out to unlock the door. He looked terribly upset and his wife's voice came rolling forward like thunder from the dark behind him, "Don't let them in, it's too late. They could be criminals." He grumbled that people should be in the house before dark and that he had been disturbed in his rest, but when he saw a handful of cigarettes or a quarter loaf of bread, a friendly visage evolved from the mean folds of cheek and jowls. "Yes, yes," he'd suddenly say looking like St. Nicholas, "it can happen, of course." Then he'd whisper confidentially, "The wife. One has to keep the wife happy, what? Hee hee." And as he turned, his hand slid behind his back where it was ready to receive the good-will bribe. It was the time-honored gesture of all Hausmeisters, waiters, and government clerks.

Mother had been searching for Aunt Leni Ullrich and Jutte. The authorities had no one registered by that name. But that meant nothing at the time. If a Hausmeister had not turned in the registration cards the housing authority had no record. Our Herr Schwartz was quick to comply and turn in his cards. It had meant for him, after all, extra ration stamps.

"When will they fix the elevator?" said Aunt Leni gasping for breath when Mother opened the door. Aunt Leni never began with a greeting, nor did she answer with a greeting. The first thing out of her mouth was a question.

"Leni! Now there you are," smiled Mother and hugged

her haggard sister. "Ah, yes, the housing authority had the address. From the Hausmeister. Two things he does perfect, turn in the names and have his hand open behind his back. And there is Jutte. My you look grown up. You are eighteen now, aren't you?" She pulled them both in, Aunt Leni with one hand, Jutte with the other. The big suitcase with the chafed sides and loose corners remained standing there. It looked fragile and had lost its shine just like Aunt Leni her-self. Mother and Aunt Leni could not be sisters, I decided. One was full of energy, one had lost it; one was blond, one was dark; one had a ready smile and laughter, the other only resignation and doubt.

"Willy, you get the suitcase," Mother ordered.

I could not lift it. Jutte had lugged it up five flights! Jutte rose immediately in my esteem. What other hidden powers lay beneath that rather skinny frame, I wondered. I dragged it, shoved it and kicked at it, until I banged it through the doors with authority showing Jutte my stuff.

"We'll put you up here in this room," I heard Mother say. "Of course I must get two straw sacks. That means finding a bribe for Schwartz. Ah, we'll manage."

We managed. The apartment had large rooms off to the right of the hallway, but as Rose and I found out on our first day, the windows were gaping holes through which wind and rain came freely and buckled the floor boards. The wallpaper with a golden curlicue design had flaked off the walls and hung in strips. Telephone wires came out of the wall but they stopped in midair as though they were on the lookout for the mysteriously lost phones. Mother had chosen the smaller back rooms to the left of the hall. The windows looking down into the courtyard still had glass in them. The pressure waves from the bombs hadn't reached that far, I guess. There was a small oven in one room. Rose and I slept on straw sacks in the room off to the left. We had one window, but there was nothing much to look at except down below among the debris scurried a lively family of rats. Mother slept in the "oven room" and Jutte's and Aunt Leni's straw sacks were also placed there. The WC was straight across from the entry and Rose and I had to maneuver through the oven room, a hallway, and the kitchen to get there. Oh, was it cold in there! It had a small ventilation window through which the wind blew with a vengeance as if to hurry the visitor along.

Mother was happy to have Aunt Leni with us. She could supervise Rose and me after school, while Mother was out hustling for a job and stealing more food. She took Jutte along.

"Jutte must go out with me. What would a young girl like that do all alone in this small apartment? It would drive any half-grown crazy."

"I'm not a half-grown anymore, Aunt Agnes," she protested. "I'm already—"

"Yes, yes, pardon me," mocked Mother. "You are a Fräulein now." She eyed her up and down critically. Jutte turned around, first left then right, to show off her woman-hood. "Well...what? You have developed I must admit. Now then, a girl having grown like you can certainly learn to hus-tle up business with me. Playtime is childlike, no?"

When it was bedtime, I was left out of the action. I was red with jealousy. Rose could stay and listen and talk with all the grown women while I—what was I supposed to do? Suck my thumb? It was four against one.

"Bedtime, Willy" they chirped. And I was pushed out of the room where I was sure interesting things were going to happen. Somehow I had to outsmart them. It drove me crazy to be so excluded. First I tried to charm Mother with my angelic smile, but all she said was, "No, no, this is for grown-ups. It's nothing for children." Then I stomped into my room and faked tears. "Let him be," I heard Jutte say when Mother made attempts to discipline me, "he will get over the problem." Finally I tried to take the high road—nose high and to bed early. I hoped they would think I was sick or something. But they went on unconcerned about my sudden psychological depression. Suddenly I had the answer: the keyhole! Through the keyhole one could scan the other side like a camera. The eye was the film that recorded the action, and the air space of the hole also carried the voices well enough. Two strikes in one! All I had to do was pull the key out when no one was looking. This key was never used anyway. Why would anyone lock the door to my room? It wouldn't be missed at all.

I peeped and I peeped, but they only sat there and chatted themselves to death. I could hear their voices but they spoke too low. I guess they didn't want to wake me.

But one time I saw. Jutte was trying on different clothes. I saw Rose dancing excitedly around. But the stupid sister of mine danced mostly in front of Jutte, in my line of vision. I hissed madly. Jutte pulled her sweater over her head and let it fall. Then she did something lower and everybody was looking and admiring and saying "it fits" and "perfect," but Rose was standing right there like a klutz. I'd kill her, for sure. Jutte was turning around like a model. The best I could see was a white, pointy garment that stuck out so far even

Rose couldn't block it. Aha, I said to myself, of course, the BH. But who cared about the Bosom Holder itself, when the more intriguing matter concerned what the Holder holds. If it hadn't been for Rose I'd have seen a lot more. Everything. I simply had to take Rose into my confidence. Maybe I could bribe her with one of my allotment of Vienna Kisses next time Mother baked them. She'd not be able to turn down such a powerful bribe.

Jutte was the exact opposite of Aunt Leni. Aunt Leni looked old. She was ten years older than Mother. She was the "unfortunate accident," Mother had mumbled whenever she talked about the poor Aunt Leni. Grandmama had not wanted any children that early. Aunt Leni had arthritis everywhere. She could barely get up from her straw sack. It was an agonizing thing to watch. And I always watched. First she'd swing her left foot over the edge, then followed the right foot, oh so slowly. You could hear the knees and ankles creak. Then she strained to sit up. There she rested, feet on the floor. She wore heavy wool socks all year, and all night long.

"What are you looking at?" she asked brusquely without even looking at me. And when I asked why she wore socks all the time, she growled, "Don't you wear socks to keep warm? I need them to keep my blood circulating in my feet. Oh the old bones. Never let your bones get to be like mine, Willy."

By the time she got all the way up, first by doubling over, then bent over like a coal miner, then rising inch by inch, groaning and creaking and complaining, I had to hustle off to school. I never knew how she managed to climb up five floors. To this day I can't remember seeing her again on the stairwell. But eventually she must have come down because Jutte had gotten married and Aunt Leni moved in with her.

Aunt Leni's clothes were dark. Even her socks were gray. Black dress, black nightdress, black shoes. Her face had the pointed nose and the thin features of Grandmama. Her eyes were blue, large round openings tinged with worry as though wondering what would happen next. Mother said that she was beautiful as a young girl and had many suitors. Grandmama, however, turned them all down, saying they were too young and had no work. The one that was approved was an older man, Ullrich. When Aunt Leni came home one day with a black eye, Grandmama kept her right there at home. And when Ullrich came to get her, Grandmama told him off in such unheard-of language that he left in an awful hurry, glad to get out of there with his hide intact. He was never seen again. But poor Aunt Leni was with child, Jutte. This all came out of Mother's mouth. Not that she talked directly to Rose and me about Aunt Leni's troubles. We were just good listeners. Our alert little ears picked up bits and pieces when Mother talked to whomever. The strange part was that Aunt Leni sometimes waxed nostalgic about Ullrich. "He was so strong," she would say, her blue eyes warming up and glowing like freshly lit candles, "muscles hard and everywhere. A beautiful man. He could lift me with one hand, like so. Yes, he could throw a heavy iron ball way up into the air and catch it on his neck. Imagine that. Healthy like an ox. Medicines? Not for him. One time he fell from a horse and split his head open. Know what he did? Took two handfuls of dirt and rubbed it into the wound! No problem."

Jutte was as fresh and blooming as her mother was ailing and wilting. I kept looking at her legs. They were so long. Starting at the ankles, which were usually wrapped in rolled-down socks—because they were too big—and looking up to where they vanished under her short skirt took an eternity. Mother called her a beanpole. She was so long and narrow. Jutte didn't like that description. Mother had to soothe her. "Now, I don't mean anything by that. Yes, yes, you are a grown girl. Where is your humor?" I knew of course that Jutte had a couple of things sticking out that had nothing to do with a beanpole. Jutte had a perpetual blush on her cheeks. Her hair fell in a dark blond curtain to her shoulders. She always reached under and flung out the curtain as if a crowd of neck lice had to be scared away and released into the immediate neighborhood, or, as if something rare and beautiful were hidden there. But I was never able to ascertain what exactly there was to see. She had a neck like any other. While her socks were too big, her skirt and dresses were too small. One had to be happy to have decent clothes, clean and whole, whether they were too small or too large didn't matter.

For myself, Mother always found clothes that were too large. The shoulders were halfway down my upper arms. The pants had to be hemmed up several inches. The belt had to have new holes punched. I preferred a belt. Suspenders kept the pants up but the waist was so wide I could look down into them and I wondered whether anyone else could. It was a floppy world for a boy like me. Again Mother had to soothe Jutte. She would, she promised, she would look for the right clothes for her, never fear.

Jutte's nose was short, a stub really. It must have come from Ullrich, Mother surmised and Aunt Leni confirmed. There was something about Jutte that made me look at her. I looked at her from top to bottom. I looked at her when she wasn't looking, from behind door jams. I stared at her at the table and watched her every move. I fixed her with my eyes involuntarily.

"What are you looking at, Willy?" she asked without really asking. "He looks so strangely at me," she told the others.

"Oh, Willy," Mother explained. "He looks at everything. He is very observant. Quiet and observant. He's just a little boy. Let him look. He's not going to devour you, is he, what?" I never had to explain myself. I wouldn't have known what to say. I would have had to think of a lie. Something like, "I think Jutte is going to explode and I want to see when it happens." Nobody would believe that, although I didn't think it would be such a lie anyway.

Then came the day that Jutte and her friend, Marlene, whom she had known from school, went over to the military prison complex on the Alsergrund. They said it was full of young German soldiers who had been caught on the last day of the war. They were only seventeen or eighteen years old and had never fired a shot at the enemy. That's what they said. They were not considered dangerous, they said. So they had many privileges as prisoners. They were all waiting to be processed and then re-introduced into society. The society needed young, strong men to build the city and the country up again. One of the privileges was that they could stand by their prison windows and wave to the pretty girls down there passing by, alone or on the arms of their mothers. They whistled and yelled down, calling for a Fräulein to become their Liebling. Then there was always laughter from the handsome blond heads at the barred windows.

Jutte and Marlene had heard of the abundance of young men waiting at the Alsergrund prison. Naturally, two plus two makes four, and Jutte and Marlene hoped to make four themselves, plus a pair of handsome ex-soldiers. For the two flushed girls it was mere fancy that drove them to walk past the windows again and again. They would never meet any one of them in person, but it was so much fun to play the game of sweet and suggestive talk. But what is for one only a game played at a distance and then dreamed about secretly during the night on a sack of straw, is for the other a preliminary stage to the real dream of love. Marlene, a rather shrunk and naturally pudgy girl who only for the grace of hard times remained trim and would later expand rapidly in direct proportion to the availability of food, and whose face resembled *Little Red Riding Hood* under stress, was of the first persuasion. Jutte was the one with real dreams. It was not long before Jutte went to the prison alone whenever she could get away under the pretense of meeting Marlene.

"I have one," she whispered one day at the table, mashing her bread into a nervous ball. Everyone had gathered around for a meager meal of fried potatoes and spinach, a slice of bread and some milk for us children, Ersatz Kaffee for the elders. Everyone looked at her. Her whisper was not a real whisper, which would only be meant for one other person next to you. It was a whisper of high distress that sounded like an alarm going on the fritz, calling for anyone to come quick and inquire. At the same time she became deep red. I observed that she was struck by the same panic that takes over at a sudden discovery of an inexplicable rash. I saw that she was at once eager to say more and to say nothing more. I wanted her to say more.

"One what?" I asked, staring into my milk glass.

There was an expectant silence around the table.

"Come on, tell us," urged Mother.

"You will not let us wonder what "one" means, what?" asked Aunt Leni.

But Jutte was silent, just looked at her bread ball and made more finger indentations in it.

"One. Well you are not sick." Mother began. "It sounds masculine. It couldn't be a dog, what?" She laughed at her own joke. We couldn't afford to feed a dog—sorry to say.

"No, no," Jutte finally burst out. "It's a boy. A man I mean. From the Alsergrund Kaserne prison."

"You don't say. A man from the Kaserne," mouthed Aunt Leni.

"Ah, an American prison guard? Wonderful. He could maybe get us some additional food," intoned my practical mother.

"How can you think of food, Aunt Agnes?" Jutte said, smacking her bread ball onto the table. "And—and he is not a prison guard, he's—he's a prisoner from the third floor." Thus began her waterfall of words that over-whelmed us all. I could barely keep up with the speed with which it drenched us. Jutte had just innocently, she said, walked by the prison when Martin, Martin was his name, called down from the third window and said, 'Liebchen, sweet as sugar, I've seen you before' and she thought he was joking, you know, like he'd say that to every girl walking by. But he said he'd seen her arm in arm with her friend, the short girl with the brown hair and the worried face. Of course he meant Marlene, but he liked *me* better, so tall and handsome, that's what he said, Martin said that—he is so blond—and talk about handsome with such a ruddy face and a big smile, and then he said he can arrange it to come down and meet her, all above board of course, he would be glad to meet her family, "All of us," just say the word. She said she'd have to ask first (and now Jutte cried a little) but he said fine, fine, no problem. Come back tomorrow, same time, and tell him, and he'll tell when we can meet. Then he said he's thinking about her (*me*, she emphasized) day and night. Then she said he asked if he could call her "sweet sugar" and she didn't know what to say, and she thought *he* thought her silence meant yes. Then he said good-bye and waved and said good-bye until tomorrow, Sugar.

Jutte's face had caught fire while her words tumbled out and over each other. I was just sitting there looking and staring. My ear was attuned to such pleading. Rose and I practiced it often on Mother. A plea it certainly was. I could clearly hear "please" and "surely you agree" and "what else do I have from life" although the words actually remained unspoken. I was curious about this Martin. I could ask him what kind of shooting he had been trained to do and how many Russians he had hoped to kill. How was he going to come down from the prison window? I've seen how people bribe with cigarettes, food, and clothing to get what they want. Mother did this every day and she talked every day about it. Everybody did it that way—the survival way. But Martin would have to bribe the prison guard. That was impossible. What had he to bribe with? How would he get around the guards who were walking up and down and around the building constantly with their guns. Martin was already a dead man.

"This is a crazy man," said Mother. "He calls you Sweet Sugar before he even knows you."

"He wants to come and meet us. Couldn't he? Oh please Aunt Agnes," Jutte begged.

"What do you think, Leni?" Mother asked Aunt Leni. But Aunt Leni didn't say much. She only mumbled something about young and foolish and how nice it is for her Jutte to have an admirer. "Now then," continued Mother, "I suppose there is no harm in inviting him, what? But how is he going to get out of the prison? Sugar he calls you, what?

Maybe he can bring us some *real* sugar. The rations give us only forty grams a week. If he can bribe the guards to get out for a couple of hours or so, maybe he can arrange for some sugar too, is it not true?"

So it was decided that Martin would come to visit. "Sugar" Jutte was on a perpetual high. It was unbearable. I hid behind a door or a table and called in a deep voice, "Sugar, Liebling, are you coming to me? I'm coming to you." But Jutte couldn't even be teased.

When Martin came it was already dark outside. Jutte hung on his arm. "This is Martin," she said, as if we didn't know it.

Martin was standing tall. His head was above everybody. He wore a perpetual smile and his chin was full of blond stubble. He had climbed down from the window to the street, he explained, on a long rope of bed sheets tied together that his friends in his cell block had gathered. It worked fine and he would use the same conveyance to climb back up to his window, unless of course "you kept me here and wouldn't let me go." He laughed out loud and squeezed Jutte with his arm that draped her shoulder as though she belonged to him. Then he announced that he brought something. After all, he couldn't come empty handed, could he? "From me and my friends in the Alsergrund Prison," he said with a playful bow. "A nice bag of sugar, stolen from the kitchen detail by Rudy Meyer, my cell mate, who always has a joke up his sleeve. He heard me call Jutte Sugar from the window and it was natural, you know, now, well, here it is."

There was laughter all around. He talked about his war experiences and how he got taken prisoner, and I hung on his words the whole time. Jutte hung on his arm and stroked him. She looked at him as though he were the only person in the room. Rose became bored and went to bed first. I knew Mother would soon send me to bed too. This had been an exciting day to beat most other days.

I lay on my straw sack staring into the darkness. Rose was already asleep a few feet away, breathing slow and deep. I could see that it was important to be some kind of a hero, even if you had been caught and put into prison. Everybody paid attention and ate up every word that came from your mouth. That's what I wanted to become, a hero. As I dreamed on in the gray-black air, I had lost track of time. Did I fall asleep for a while? But suddenly my eyes were wide and on high alert. My colorless night vision made out the outlines of the window. Rose was a dark lump on her straw bed. And there was the door. Through that door a rapid, rhythmic noise percolated, a kind of song I'd never heard before, with deep grunts and high-pitched calls like a bird in distress. I was up in a flash. For the sake of research I left my warm blankets and braved the cool night air. I stuck my left eyeball into the key hole. Nothing doing. The darkness required both eyes. I opened the door with utmost care. Now the grunts achieved a note of desperation. There seemed to be an urgency in it as though a vile deed had to be done before anyone came. But I had already arrived, the invisible witness in the dark. Poor Jutte was gasping. Then I realized Jutte was on the verge of being killed. Martin was not the handsome young captured soldier he pretended to be but a crazy man out to kill people like Jutte, maybe all of us. The prison story was all a hoax. It was a lie that stank to heaven. Even Mother fell for it. Where was Mother, anyway? And where was Aunt Leni? Their straw sacks were empty. Had they already been killed and disposed of? I had to think of myself and Rose. We had to rescue Jutte and ourselves. Grab her and run down the five flights of stairs screaming for help and pounding on Hausmeister

Schwartz's door. But how could we immobilize Martin long enough to get away? Rose had to be consulted for the answer.

"Rose," I whispered into her ear. "Rose, wake up. Jutte is in trouble. Are you awake?"

"Whaaa—" she yawned. "Jutte in trouble?"

"She's being killed by Martin. Come on we've got to do something."

"Killed?" she nearly yelled. But I held her mouth.

We stood by the crack of the door in our pajamas. I had bent down low. Rose peered into the glum room above me. The murder was still going on. Jutte was still alive. I could tell by her desperate tweaks and chirps and her painful "ohs." We had to act now.

"Rose," I said. "I jump on Martin and hold him around his throat and you pull Jutte out and tell her to run down to the Hausmeister."

"I don't know," she said. "I don't think she's getting killed. I think they are playing a game. Let's watch a little more." Rose seemed fascinated by the nocturnal scene of thrashing bodies, screams, grunts, gasps, and what not.

"Are you crazy?" I said. "This doesn't look like a game and therefore it isn't a game. I am going in." I said this bravely, but I didn't really know what to do. I had been abandoned by my own sister. "Here I go."

"No," yelled Rose, and tried to hold me back. But she had forgotten to whisper. Did she want to save me? Was she trying to protect me? Did her brother love come through?

Her cry had an immediate reaction from the straw sack where Martin had pounded Jutte and Jutte had been defending herself. Everything stopped. Already, my charge from the door was effective. I was flying through the air to pounce on the naked back of Martin when I heard Jutte's lament.

"Yikes, eeek!" screeched Jutte. "What are you doing? Oh God. They were watching us. Oh God."

"You will not kill us!" I screamed. "Get back to your prison and never, never come back. If you do I shoot you. I shoot you." And I pulled on his neck and then his hair to get him off Jutte. But then suddenly Jutte's words came to me, and then Rose's, about this being a game.

Martin shook me off, and laughed so hard I could see his stomach heaving. But Jutte was mad as could be. She had her bed sheet pulled all the way up to her mouth.

"Go back to bed, oh please," she pleaded. "This is nothing for you two. You are too young. Oh God. What will

Aunt Agnes think?"

"Yes, little man. Go to bed," said Martin laughing. "Someday you will—well—when you are older—don't worry. Jutte is safe with me. I personally guarantee that no harm will come to her. She's too beautiful and sweet for that. Like sugar." Then he bent over Jutte, still laughing, and tried to kiss her. But she only lamented, "oh, they ruined everything."

Martin came again and again. And every time he brought us some specialty. "Directly from the best post-war kitchen in the neighborhood," he said smiling and dropped his gift on the table. There was Wurst, then flour, another time, powdered sugar. One time Mother asked for vanilla sugar. And Martin brought that too. What could I do? Jutte seemed to have acquired a permanent smile except when she looked directly at me. When Martin came to us Jutte's straw sack was placed in the kitchen and Mother and Aunt Leni slept in their usual places. My days of learning more of the games they played were already over, before they had really begun. I tried to sneak through the oven room to spy on the kitchen games. But Mother always caught me at the door. I pleaded toilet needs. "Go to bed. March!" she ordered.

"Fine," I told her with a fake pout, "I'll just have to wet my bed."

"Go on," she said unconcerned. "If you want your little posterior decorated with the prints of my hand." Mother always knew how to cure my ills. It was either her hand prints, or the threat of no Vienna Kisses in the near future.

Roland Gööck's Recipe
Vienna Kisses

Step 3

Finely grate 350 grams of hazelnuts and
stir into egg-sugar-vanilla mixture…

❧❧❧ 5 ❧❧❧

A girl can goad a boy, or a boy a girl, into the hazelnut
bushes. But beware of the busy, watchful squirrels.

In a northwesterly direction, on the outskirts of the city,
is Nußdorf. Leading to Nußdorf is, of course, the Nußdorfer
Straße. Just beyond Nußdorf begins the Wienerwald. Yes,
the very one of love and wine and bucolic scenery that none
other than Strauß immortalized in his *Tales of the Vienna
Woods*. But by way of Nußdorf (Nutvillage in free transla-
tion), isn't the only path into the Vienna Woods. One can
take the Electric in a more northerly direction out to
Währing and begin hiking immediately. If one was a young
male or a young female in the early postwar period, hiking

74

into the Vienna Woods only took five minutes, it wasn't that Viennese girls and boys didn't like hiking or, God forbid, didn't like their Vienna Woods. It was because their progress was halted by that rare obstruction called Währinger Bad, an open-air swimming pool. It assumed priority over hiking and the Vienna Woods. One was, after all, a young male or female. The lovely pool was built with Ami (American) dollars, obviously as a morale builder for the young and deprived population. Ask anyone; it was a highly moral place, even though these very deprived youths had accumulated a high degree of depravity in their thoughts. Love was thick in the air and choking off intelligent conversations. There was intense male ogling from behind a towel or a friend's back or when gasping for breath doing the crawl stroke. The beautiful sex, equally ogling, lounged on the grass, oiled themselves, dipped into the water occasionally, giggled and judged the performances all around. There were never more young athletes assembled doing handstands, pushups, somersaults, soccer juggling, funny dives, and other horseplay for these hungry eyes to judge. Girls forever fussed with the upper and lower edges of their swimming outfits as if to lure attention to those parts, so forbiddingly and yet so attractively hidden there.

In their painful frustration the boys found refuge in the cold sparkling waters of the pool that chlorinated the body and cleansed it of impurities and embarrassment immediately upon entering. There were always more boys in the water than girls. It was humanity on the rebound. It manifested itself in the hearts and minds of the young and in the display of pale, still skinny bodies at poolside.

Or, one could head out directly west to Hütteldorf, the home turf of the soccer club Rapid, the first to win the championship of the new era. The pitch had been built at the edge of the Vienna Woods. After a game the fans could cool their hot blood in the shade of the great forest. Here played the real heroes of the war. They even showed up one time for a match while the bombs rained upon the city.

The major electric streetcar lines to the outer districts such as Nußdorf were the first ones to be repaired and put into service. The outskirts had always had a special attraction for the people of Vienna. They were the gateways to the great out-of-doors where one went for a picnic, a hike, or on a search for mushrooms. After debarking the Electric, the wanderer would first pass the rich villas with their elaborate wrought iron gates and full foliage of grapes and hazelnut bushes before entering the Vienna Woods proper. The

Americans, quite naturally fond of being from the "west" liked to stick proudly with that denomination. It was to no ones surprise that they occupied the western portion of the city and appropriated choice properties for their generals, the villas just mentioned. The pillaging Russians, coming from the east, occupied the fertile flatlands and the small farm communities abutting the Danube.

It was good to live in the American Sector, the Ami Sector. The Amis were kind and the streets were safe. The Russians, however, were suspicious and the patrolling soldiers looked mean-spirited and dangerous. They could whip around their rifles and mow you down without another thought. They simply grabbed children and sent them to Siberia on the next train east. If you wanted to get away from your mean parents or a mean brother or sister, or you'd think you'd never make it in school to the disgrace of your hardworking mother, all you had to do was step over the demarcation line and say, hey, Russki, here I am, take me to Siberia. But if you loved your mother like I did and you craved her cooking and baking of Vienna Kisses, you stayed on this side of the line, the Ami Sector.

The Amis not only favored the fancy villas but they also moved right into the palais of Count S, hero of the defeat of the Hungarian hordes in the 19th century, and established their consulate there. This was where my friend Otto and I glimpsed the largest Christmas tree of all time. It was decorated with bright glass balls and lit garlands, stars and tinsel. We stood on the street with our faces pressed against the iron bars of the fence and stared into that dreamland that seemed to exist behind the huge balcony windows of the Palais.

It wasn't just the giant, glittering Christmas tree that amazed us. People seemed to hover around it like fairies, moving in and out of the picture with perfect ease. The women appeared like creatures from a different planet. They seemed to float about in white shoulder-free gowns with a glass in hand, their angelic hair bouncing on pale flesh, and with their chests strapped high and pointed forward like an offering. I've already heard Mother gossip about the American women. "How they prance with the bosoms, look," she huffed, "how they douse themselves in perfume and shave their underarms as if they have nothing else to do." Such "shaving" talk came with the immediate warning, "if you shave naturally-occurring hair you will have to shave until you die because if you don't the hair will grow back with a vengeance, ten times its thickness, ten times its length." My mind conjured images of hair pouring out from the armpits. It would have to be combed every day and braided and layered thickly around the waist, unless cut and shaved away. The women Otto and I ogled had definitely shaved, and we swore we could smell their perfume all the way to here on the snowy street as we held on to the cold steel bars with cramping fingers. I said that I smelled nuts with chocolate. But Otto insisted otherwise. "Don't be dumb. It's roses. They like roses. You must be thinking of cookies, aren't you?" I was, actually. They had to have cookies up there, didn't they? I doubt that they had Vienna Kisses. But any cookie would have done for me.

The villas in "Nutvillage" had large front and back yards. Fences were old wooden slat fences. Most were in disrepair. But they had blackberries, hazelnut bushes and grapevines growing over and through them. In summer they grew so thick that nothing of the yard, let alone the villa beyond, could be seen. Otto liked to say "he'd been around." He said that under those bushes, perfectly concealed, boys laid with girls, girls with boys. Otto was a year older than I and therefore he knew a lot. But we were in the same class and lived only two streets from each other. He had an older brother, Heinrich, from whom he had probably heard much of the stuff that he claimed to have been "around." I didn't like Heinrich. He was fifteen and sported a little mustache and carried his nose so high I could see into his nostrils. One time he showed us his rifle—a BB rifle—and when I begged him to let me hold it he said, "OK, just once." So I took it and aimed directly at him pretending to shoot his head off. Heinrich flew off his rocker. He stomped his feet and called me a dirty name. "Ignoramus," he yelled. Well, I wasn't an ignoramus. I should have pulled the trigger when I had the chance. But Otto and I were good friends. His mother spoke Russian, and his father was a judge. Mother said they could come in handy sometime. If I got caught by a Russian soldier Otto's mother could get me off the hook, and if I got into some other trouble the father could defend me in a court. That's what Mother said. For myself, I really liked Otto. He always shared stuff with me, and he helped me cheat in school. Otto had a brain. His head was already bigger than anyone else's, so all this smartness could fit into it. I had a smaller head, but I was stronger than he and faster. You could say Otto called the shots and I carried them out. By that I mean Otto had all these great ideas which he told me about, but I ended up giving a "but" here and a "maybe" there. Pretty soon he and I had the idea shaved and trimmed down to where we could actually attempt to carry out a deed. It wasn't that he let me carry the load alone. He came right along with me to the edge of the precipice, as it were, and risked everything. Maybe Otto had come to the brink once too many times, because he had a tick in his right eye. He squeezed it shut and grunted at the same time. When our excitement rose, his eye-shutting habit increased in proportion. "Let's—" shut-shut-grunt, "—do it," he would announce.

School was out at two and Mother wasn't going to be home until five, as usual. The news about girls and boys under the bushes in Nutvillage had circulated for a while but it had never dawned on us to be concerned. At ten or eleven, Otto's age, our pastime consisted of searching for treasure in the heaps of rubble that were everywhere, or playing soccer with a rag ball, with an abandoned entryway serving as goal. But Otto, the progressive, had an idea.

"Let's go to Nußdorf and watch the action," he said one day.

"What action?" I countered.

"The action under the bushes. We can hide easily and

81

watch their games." He got excited already and his eye twitched.

Now I knew what games he referred to. The same games Jutte and Martin had been engaged in. I had never been able to make out what the killing scene really was all about. My curiosity had been poked awake.

"But where will we hide, so that if we are found out we can run like hell and not get beat up by the big boys," I said, visualizing a mad scramble and dash up alongside the moving Electric and jumping on.

"We'll scout it out. Besides, before they can chase us they'd have to get dressed. They wouldn't run out into the wide-open street with their pants at their ankles, would they?"

Pants at their ankles? Why would their pants be at their ankles? I didn't question Otto further. He must have prior knowledge about such pants that were hanging around the ankles in front of a girl.

Otto must have had bad info. We walked a long way up the Nußdorfer Straße, passing villa after villa. The bushes were loaded with hazelnuts and the Wienerwald squirrels had come all the way down to the villas to fill their cheeks. There were no girls or boys to be seen anywhere. There were no people, period. It seemed the whole street was abandoned, like just before a bombing attack. It was a disappointment, to say the least. But I could do one thing. I could gather some nuts and stuff my pockets with them like the squirrels stuffed their cheeks. Mother would be pleased. I had done something very useful, she'd say, and kiss me with a noisy smack, Vienna style, on the cheek. Otto saw my point. We parted the bushes and picked and munched hazelnuts alternately until we bulged in three places, two pockets and our stomachs. Suddenly Otto motioned me to be quiet and stop moving. He pointed ahead into the thicket right before us. In the stillness (I had stopped chewing) a groaning and a whimpering could be heard not unlike the song I had been accustomed to with Jutte and "Sugar" Martin. Inch by careful inch we zeroed in on the couple under the bushes. What I finally saw burnt itself indelibly into my mind. I would never ever be caught in such a ridiculous pose, where someone could see me from a hidden observation point with my pink behind exposed and moving up and down like a struggling swimmer. As Otto had said, pants were at the ankles. The girl was throwing her head left and right, squealing and saying oh-no's over and over. In one glorious moment I glimpsed the whiteness of her breast through the fingers of her swimmer boyfriend. I glanced over at Otto. His vision was glued to the action while his one twitchy eye was in overdrive and his grunts audible over the noise of the hazelnut lovers. But what made the scene come to an abrupt end weren't his grunts, not the rustling leaves we touched, but a squirrel who single-mindedly and acrobatically collected his allocation of nuts. Trouble was that he had to do it right there above the drowning couple where he called attention to himself balancing from branch to branch in search of another nut. The young lady noting the scrambling creature in her convulsions also glimpsed Otto's one-eyed visage peering at her from his vantage point. He must have appeared to her as the Hunchback of Notre Dame, or Jack the Ripper, or some other escaped convict, because she let out a scream that went to our bones through muscle and flesh without delay. Her lover, however, took it as her unique expression of love and tried even harder to swim to the end of the pool.

Well, Otto and I took off as fast as our young legs could carry us. We hopped on the Electric just now leaving the station. We were safe. Red-cheeked and with full pockets of nuts and with a new appreciation of girl-boy relations we headed home.

I presented my take to Mother and cashed in on one version of the Vienna Kiss.

Roland Gööck's Recipe
Vienna Kisses

Step 4
Grind 1 tsp of coffee into fine powder and
stir into mixture…

A nose is not a nose is not a nose. But the aroma of real
coffee does not discriminate among them.

War wounds were clearly on the mend when that inde-
fatigable class of humanity, the businessmen's class, began
to assert itself again. While heretofore personal survival
took the top spot in their members' list of priorities—the
eventual return to their calling was never far from their
mind. It took no more than five or six months after the last
bomb fell, and after the Allies had completed the final divi-
sion of the great city into four sectors with checkpoints,
demarcation lines, and rotating administrators, before their
sense of profit claimed the rightful leadership position

among thoughts and actions of daily life. The mind of a businessman runs rampant during a temporary lull when the scrambling for the daily bread could be postponed 'till tomorrow. What would they do in the future? Somewhere money could be made, property accumulated, people hired to do the actual work. What were the needs of the masses? What could he sell them? Would he take only cash, or would he be willing to barter? Perhaps more barter than cash in the beginning. Perhaps begin with installment plans. But collections could be a problem even if that burden were passed on to the sales force.

The sales force. Ah, the headaches of hiring a sales force! Work permits, reliability, extension of credit, inventory dilution, physical fitness, the will and the energy to work for an honest Mark (soon to be a Schilling), tax compliance.

Herr Georgye Saleta, the Greek, and Herr Mordecai Feldmann, the bent Jew, decided to combine their expertise as businessmen. They had been successful before, each in his own field, when the Nazis suddenly had pulled the rug out from under them. Saleta, not yet married, not even engaged, had gone into hiding because his leanings were communist (he didn't like the alternative, Fascism). The stocky man with boxer shoulders and large face highlighted by a flattened nose smartly abandoned his wholesale distribution business from one day to the next. Feldmann, single (his family had moved away long before the Anschluß) and determined to make a fortune, had held out with unreasonable optimism—dealing in clothing for men, women and children—until one night his store window was smashed, the interior ransacked and plundered, and during the next night he was dragged from his bed, told to pack, and was shipped off to a holding camp whence he was to be resettled. He was then a wiry man with a straight back, long nose, and a full shock of black hair. But Feldmann was put to work in back-breaking labor. His tall frame bent until he had shrunk six inches by the time he was liberated. His nose seemed to protrude farther from his emaciated face; his hair had thinned and turned white. He was no longer a handsome man. Only his alert penetrating eyes and his acute business sense remained from his former life.

Saleta and Feldmann had met in the city's newly established Office for Commerce and Business Registration. It was hastily propped up in a former schoolhouse whose classrooms, aligned like insect chambers left and right along endless halls, served this bureaucracy, indeed would have served any bureaucracy, well. The former classrooms still smelled of paper, ink and dust even after months of abandonment. The roof leaked, crumbling walls were braced with timbers, plaster rained from the ceilings like snow, wallpaper still hung in shreds. But new businesses had to be registered, tax forms printed and distributed, and hiring lists posted in the large entrance hall through which boisterous and eager kids once stormed to get to their cells of knowledge.

Saleta and Feldmann hashed it out over many cups of evil tasting Ersatz kaffee. Finally, they incorporated as Saleta-Feldmann, GmbH. Sales, Service and Distribution of Ladies Wear. They posted a job ad: Salespeople wanted! Women preferred. Apply in person at Am Kai, Number 56. The business was up and struggling when Mother first saw the poster.

Mother dressed us in our finest. That meant there couldn't be holes or frizzy cuffs, there couldn't be a speck of dirt on us anywhere. Our hair got combed until our heads looked unnatural. I felt like a doll that had been dipped head first into a washtub and then polished.

I protested. "What are we going to do there?"

"Hush. I need a job and they give jobs to women who

have children to feed. It looks good to have you there. Shows that I can take care of children, that I am a responsible woman without a husband anymore." Her tone did not leave us a chance to argue. It was a fact. We were going and that was that. Rose displayed one of her famous frowns.

"You get rid of your frown! Hear me, Rose? Nobody gives me a job with a daughter who frowns and makes herself look ugly."

"I am not ugly," whined Rose.

"You smile nicely, then you are not ugly. That is very simple."

Rose frowned even more. I made a point of grinning at her, bearing all my teeth and pulling the corners of my mouth far out. "Grin like this," I said.

"Now that's ugly, like a toad," she said waving her dangerous forefinger. I was certain she was going to poke me soon from behind. I had to keep an eye on her.

"Here is what you will say," Mother's briefing went on. "First you say a nice Guten Tag, hear me? With a smile! Is that clear? Then if you are asked anything you answer quietly and clearly. They will ask who will take care of you while I work. I will say, 'my sister. She is very competent in spite of her arthritis,' I will say."

"But Aunt Leni doesn't know anything," Rose said.

"Quiet. She is doing the best she can. Here you will say, yes, Aunt Leni is very competent."

We arrived at Saleta-Feldmann, GmbH. It had a small door and a tiny dirty display window with nothing on display.

As soon as we opened the door we were hit with the strongest smell of coffee I had ever experienced. Even Mother was shocked. She breathed in the aroma as though it were the smell of heaven.

"Now that is coffee," she said just loud enough to be heard.

"Ah, yes. Coffee," said a deep voice from behind a counter. We didn't see anyone at first. But then the man stood up. He was bent over at the waist. He looked like a scarecrow. I must have stared at him too long because he tried to smile. But all I could see were brown teeth and the longest nose.

Mother turned to us. "What do you say?" she hissed.

"Guten Tag!" Rose and I said in unison.

"Looks like you know good coffee when you smell it, Gnädige Frau. What is your wish?"

So, Mother applied for the job as commission saleswoman. She pleaded her case with a passion. She pointed to us. She said we needed better nourishment. She said she had to take care of her ailing sister and her daughter. She said her sister was competent in taking care of the children while she would be out working. She asked us without a hesitation in her voice and without the redness of shame, "What do you say, Rose and Willy, isn't she good?"

"Aunt Leni is very co—co—pentent, Mister," I stammered.

"He means competent, Herr Feldmann."

"Come tomorrow at ten o'clock sharp," said Feldmann earnestly. Do you have a suitcase? Bring a suitcase. Herr Saleta will give you the works and show you how to pack a suitcase. Have a cup of coffee. Herr Saleta has connections. This is rare coffee! I have nothing for the children. I am sorry. Here. What do you think?"

"Oh, Wunderbar!" exclaimed Mother. "The best cup I've had, Oh in so long a time. Vienna without good coffee is almost impossible to fathom. Hmmmm—"

"Perhaps later we can strike a barter, once you have established your salesmanship, eh?" Feldmann sat back down and bent over some papers.

Mother finished her cup. "I would do almost anything to

get coffee like this instead of the terrible Ersatzkaffee. Yes, I can think that you will not be disappointed in me. Thank you."

The next day Mother came home with a stuffed suitcase. Everyone gathered around to see. Even I was permitted to stay. She lifted the lid and the oh's and ah's came from all around. Aunt Leni said, "how crazy, how crazy" over and over when Mother lifted the silky underwear from the depths of the suitcase and turned them this way and that way. There were pink, white, and yellow underpants, brassieres, underskirts, nightgowns, and slips. Everything was thoroughly inspected and admired to the last stitch.

"Crazy is this," laughed Aunt Leni. "Who would wear something like this? Isn't it only for those who walk the line?"

"What are you saying, Leni," protested Mother. "This is the latest. Every young woman wants to wear this. They have been deprived of such indulgence for too long. They'll go like warm rolls, I tell you. And not just young women. My age, too. Ha, what do you think?"

"I like it too," said Jutte. "It feels so good. So soft and cool and attractive, no? Aunt Agnes, can I have one of these, please?"

"Don't be ridiculous. This is what I have to sell! Starting tomorrow. Somebody has to bring in the money, isn't that true?"

Thus, I had begun to become an expert in women's undergarments. One day, in late August, I even went with Mother on her sales route. In and out of shops we went; up and down factory staircases; in and out of government office buildings. Wherever women worked, wherever women had their private changing rooms, lunch rooms, and water closets, that's where we lugged the heavy suitcase. I shouldn't say we. I tried it only once. Confident in my strength I offered to carry the suitcase up to the third floor where the women had gathered for their lunch break. It nearly broke my back.

"Not quite as strong as you think, what?" said Mother. "Just think, my son, I carry this thing up and down hundreds of times, every day! I wonder what it will do to my hands. They already look like a laborer's. Not to speak of my back. Come on. Let's make a sale, what?"

So I went in with her into the lunch room. The women gathered around, chatting all at once and giggling and whooping as they held the little pants and the bras to themselves, checking for size, and turning around for approval.

Mother kept pushing for a sale. "Very beautiful," she would say with earnest eyes, "doesn't this feel good?" and "wait 'till your gallant sees this," or "you can still grow into this you know with a little more fattening up there." Finally, she'd put the squeeze on. "What do you think this is, a rag? This is most reasonably priced, I tell you, barely above my cost. What do you think? I have to make a living too. And you can buy on an installment plan. I'll be back every week to collect your weekly payment."

Mother was good. The flimsy things practically flew out of her hands and the suitcase. Soon she added a second suitcase. And she had never held a job. As the wife of an officer before and during the early part of the war she had had it easy. Suddenly she had become the top saleslady for Saleta-Feldmann, GmbH. The once despised communist and the one-time "dirty Jew," in an ironic switch, became the employers of a military wife who had once been privileged and had belonged to the oppressor class.

I knew when Mother had a good week. Coffee, real coffee, with that strong aroma was served. She said a small bag of coffee cost her the profit from six pair of underpants. It was extortion, she cried. But oh, she did like coffee. Only once did I help grind down the beans to a coarse powder with a small hand mill. It was a boring task, besides I derived no benefit from coffee at all. And 1 declined to grind anymore until Mother said this: "Don't forget the recipe for Vienna Kisses calls for a little bit of coffee. Now, with real coffee for additional flavor they'll taste just that much better."

Coffee and women's underwear! What else had the future in store for me?

Roland Gööck's Recipe
Vienna Kisses

Step 5
Finely grate 50 grams of unsweetened baking chocolate.
Mix together with all other ingredients…

 7

Schoko for the victors and the vanquished. Schoko for the prevention of war.

I contend that the transition from a defeated and desperate people to a society of optimistic, hard working, and cheerful citizens can be easily achieved with the free and abundant distribution of chocolate. It's like manna from heaven, it's the drug of the masses (next to football), it's the stiller of hunger, the satisfier of desires, the energizer of athletes, and the calmer of excited soldiers. Give soldiers on all sides loads and loads of chocolate (schoko to us) and you can kiss wars goodbye. Only Americans seem to understand the value of chocolate. An Ami soldier can count on a

Hershey bar in his ration. That's enough to win them a rep-
utation of kindness, benevolence, and fairness. Generous
amounts of schoko should be a part of any negotiations. It
should be the first part. Hand a tray with Schoko treats
around the room and I guarantee peace.

When Otto and I had a craving for schoko— which was
about seven days a week— and when our mothers and aunts
and the benevolent ladies of the Salvation Army couldn't
come up with any, we took it upon ourselves to plead at the
door from which poured forth the keepers of an allegedly
unlimited supply. We laid siege to the exit of the "Palais des
Americains," the Palais of the old Count S., the very same
facility of Christmas tree fame that pursued us into our
dreams along with the Christmas elves in shoulder-free
dresses dancing around it, cigarettes dangling professional-
ly from their lips, and sipping from bubbly glasses.

The Salvation Army women in their trim blue uniforms
with red "S" on their lapels and caps at a rakish angle on
their heads gathered in a half circle on busy street corners to
sing of the Lord's Love and Compassion with bursts of
white breath clouds rising to heaven in the crisp winter air.
They had learned how to sing and smile at the same time.
Rich passers-by would drop a Pfennig or two into the small

shoebox in their midst.

"It's just another job," Mother had explained when I stopped to observe. "They get ration cards and a portion of the day's donation."

I loved watching their mouths move in unison and their hands wringing. Their doleful eyes locked on to passers-by like powerful magnets until they felt obliged to drop something into the collection box. Something. After all, it could well be that the Lord was watching, and one didn't want to be caught in the sin of hard heartedness. And what man could resist the smile and the pleading looks of the singing sisters and not dig deep to produce a little donation. It calmed both heart and conscience.

My angelic face, as Mother liked to call it (to the chagrin of my sister Rose), regularly caught the attention of at least one of the Salvation Army's Ladies at the corner of Ring Straße and Schottengasse, and with a quick hand motion that lady would beckon me over and squeeze a piece of schoko into my hand. Mother was amazed. "What do you know," she said smiling, "your angelic visage made her do it." Then we'd share the piece in blissful silence. But Otto, who had nothing in his face that reminded one of an angel—it was more like a rumpled soccer ball with a rip where his eye twitched—even *he* could get a piece of schoko out of them.

In spite of the generosity of the Salvation Army Ladies, perhaps because of the hit and miss of such chocolate handouts, and because our bodies screamed for more, Otto and I staked out the "Palais des Americains." We learned quickly that Wednesdays, Fridays, and Saturdays were the big days. The huge double doors, flanked by two white-helmeted guards with rifles, opened and the good, victorious Amis in dress uniforms emerged in groups or arm in arm with the beauties of the Christmas tree variety. We were quick to act. We ran up to the emerging and bewildered men, sucked in our cheeks a bit to simulate emaciation, and pleaded "Schoko? Schoko?" But all we got were green packages of chewing gum. We couldn't even handle the quantity of chewing gum which they threw at us. We felt like dogs chasing the bouncing green packages, as they laughed their heads off. We were stray dogs to them, or at least a pest in human form you could keep at bay with tokens like that.

"No schoko," I said to Otto sadly. "What's the matter with them?"

"Willy, I've got it," Otto said, putting on a sort of dismissive air, but his eye was twitching with excitement. "They don't know what schoko is. They think maybe that schoko is our word for chewing gum. My Papa told me that their schoko is called Hershey. Let's hit them up for Hershey." He grunted once and was off to confront the next couple emerging.

"Hershey? Hershey?" he cried.

"Naw," said the Ami man. "Here, have some gum." And he threw a package into the street.

But we were undeterred. We kept it up. Then, on Friday next, it seemed they had caught on. Perhaps a general in charge of public relations had ordered to dish out Hershey bars. Let's show them what we are made of, he must have said. We ended up with eight Hershey bars and only five chewing gum packs! The feeling of having succeeded! It was worth sharing and off we ran toward home. But at the street corner where we had to part, we stood in silence, carefully unwrapped one of the gently curved bars, nearly fainted from the rich brown smell that escaped, and then devoured it limb by limb with a distinct air of pagan reverence. Otto was about to unwrap his next bar but I told him not to be stupid. Save it, I said. But he couldn't help himself. Right. I understood Otto. He was the first schoko

addict I knew. I've heard of people who deny similar crav-
ings openly, but secretly act like Otto. They'd let a sister cry
bitter tears, or let a grandmother beat them over the head
with their walking stick, but they would not give up that
smooth, precious concoction, the entry ticket to bliss. For
myself—I was a good boy—I rushed up the five flights and
into the door to tell of my good fortune (minus the one I
already ate and minus the one I kept hidden for later storage
under my straw sack). Even Rose, in spite of her dangerous
forefinger for which she should be made to pay a penalty,
got her share, thanks mostly to Mother. "Sharing is surviv-
ing," she kept preaching, "as long as it doesn't go too far
beyond family. These are hard times—that you know, don't
you?" To be fair, I thought, Rose should at least get less. I
have the blue bruises on my ribs to show for my—well, my
good heart.

When it came to schoko I turned into a hunter-gatherer-
saver, a human squirrel. Small, medium and large pieces
found their way under my straw sack. At the foot end I laid
them, orderly and ready like a phalanx of warriors, organ-
ized by age. They were treats, bargaining chips, prizes. For
a favor I promised schoko and I always delivered.

"Hey, Otto," I said one day when I knew his bicycle had been fixed. "How about a spin?" Lucky Otto had found the bike, smashed and bent, under a pile of rubble he was exploring in the Berggasse.

"Well, uh," he stammered as his eye twitched, "they are still working on it." He meant his mustachioed brother and his father-judge.

"I'd be willing to part with a fine chunk of you-know-what for—well, you know what I want." I made his eye twitch faster and his grunts came from his throat when I mentioned the magic word. The deal was made and consummated soon after.

When I wanted to know the details of Jutte's games with POW Martin, I said to Rose, "Rose," I said sweetly, "you want some schoko?"

"Sure," she said eagerly falling into my trap. "Show me what's in your hand?"

I showed her. A full half of a Hershey chocolate bar, still in its original wrapping. "Uh-uh," I shook my head when she reached out. "First things first—"

And so I found out that Jutte liked wrestling. "They roll and they roll around each other," explained Rose. "And they laugh so dumb the whole time."

"And then?" I asked.

"They kiss and stop rolling. They do a lot of kissing."

"And then?"

"What then? I don't know. They wrestle again. This time completely under the blanket as if they try to throw each other off the straw sack. Now give me the chocolate. Come on!"

"All right," I said. I had a little more insight than before. It might come in handy someday in a conversation at school.

Mother, Rose, Jutte, Aunt Leni were all fond of chocolate. I was too, but I had my craving under control. But when it came to Mother's baking I had as little control as a dog smelling a bone. It wasn't my fault that most things Mother baked had schoko in it. When my contributions didn't suffice, Mother had to look elsewhere.

"Not all chocolate lends itself to baking," she announced one day to my profound surprise. "What you need is baking chocolate. That will give off the right flavor." What, I wondered, had she done with the schoko I had so generously shared? Did she hoard it like I did? Actually that would not be too far fetched. I knew she hoarded silver coins when Austria began issuing its own currency, the

Schilling. I had discovered how she secretly stuffed something into an old voluminous purse and hid it at the bottom of her closet. And when she wasn't there and Aunt Leni was napping on her straw sack (she snored reassuringly), I dug out her purse. I could hardly lift it. Wow! It was pregnant with coin, ready to burst. I felt like a pirate finding the long sought treasure chest. This was a secret worth keeping, not to be shared with anyone, not even for ten bars of schoko. Mother and I had an unspoken agreement. Her secret was my secret. My secret was her secret. Whenever I looked at my mother, that purple purse full of "gold" jumped out in my mind. Still today, after all those years, I can feel the smooth leathery bag. I can smell the mustiness of that dark closet corner, and I can still feel my red face burn as I struggled to keep my fingers from lifting just one coin. One lousy coin would be OK, wouldn't it? Who'd notice? Then, Aunt Leni's sudden break in her snoring—the sudden panic and the sweaty guilt of having been caught red-handed by the awakening sawmeister—overwhelmed me as I knelt praying at the altar of Mammon in a handbag.

So, if ordinary schoko wouldn't do, how did Mother manage to acquire baking chocolate? Was it Frau Tomes who had connections? Perhaps Saleta and Feldmann, men of vast scrounging talent, sold her some. Were the Kaffeeklatsches at the widow Kowalski her source? How about Riedl, the black-clad undertaker, he of the suit with the shiny elbows and the sheen on his seat? If he didn't get paid for his corpses in currency, perhaps he was paid in goods, like schoko. I could see that a well-prepared corpse could command a needed supply of something. Didn't Riedl have a well rounded midsection? His hands and fingers were fleshy smooth. I imagined them embalming the body of the corpse with even gentle strokes. There was always a hint of goose bumps and imaginings of flaccid corpses wandering about when he would make gestures to shake your hand. So where did he get his more than necessary nourishment? Riedl explained it himself in so many words when he partook in a Kaffeklatsch.

"Let me tell you about my corpse today, my dear ladies," he would begin. Then he would lean on his elbow, lay his fleshy hand alongside his cheek, and sigh with satisfaction. The ladies listened carefully because if he had had a fine corpse, Herr Riedl would suddenly fish from one of his vast black pockets a treat that would take their breath away. Only the widow Kowalski would keep her composure. She knew that deeper yet in his pockets was hidden a

108

special surprise for her, for her alone.

"What a fine corpse it was; a beautiful coffin, black with golden trim; pallbearers decked out in perfect black, and behind them I, the organizer. The organizer, that's me. Oh yes. They couldn't do without me."

At this point his other hand was already fishing in his side pocket.

"Now, the widow was a tall lady, walking as straight as an arrow, head held high, like so." He stretched his double chin way out. "Seemed like nothing could make her break down, what?" His hand rose slowly out of his pocket. "But then at the hole, that's where the corpse turned from fine to beautiful. I would say it was a class A corpse. I gave the farewell at the edge of the hole and I could see the tall-walking widow melt away in agony and tears. Beautiful, what? She loved her corpse after all."

Then Riedl sighed again and pulled his hand free. Buried in his pocket had been schoko for Mother, coffee beans for Frau Tomes, and—gasp!—a little bottle of rum for the ecstatic and blushing Kowalski, his reason for coming here in the first place.

Herr Riedl was the darling of the party, of course. He laughed his cheek-shaking laugh, he reached out with his fleshy hands as if to say, isn't this a fine Kaffee and Kuchen party, eh?

As far as I was concerned schoko was the main ingredient for Vienna Kisses. It gave them flavor. It gave them an addictive aura. It gave them an unforgettable aroma, intensified during the baking step. And, lest I forget, it produced an involuntary high. One wanted to kiss someone, hug someone, slap someone on the back. I kissed Mother, Mother kissed me. Rose kissed Mother, Mother kissed Rose. Rose poked me—gently for once, and I puckered up, plunging my wet and dripping lips squarely into Rose's face. Laughter erupted all around. They weren't called Vienna Kisses for nothing.

There are kisses and there are kisses. There's the pastry kiss and there's the real kiss, like the one, a long time later, I planted on the lips of Inge of the Hörl Park—

Roland Gööck's Recipe
Vienna Kisses

Step 6
Preheat oven to 300° F.
Form 1 inch dough balls using two teaspoons
dipped in cold water for easy handling.
Place the balls on a greased cookie sheet about 3 inches
apart and indent each one with the wet tip of the little fin-
ger. Bake for about 15 minutes.
Fill indentations with marmalade or tart jam.

 8

A 15-minute kiss, heating up to 300 degrees.

It used to be a fine neighborhood. Tall five-story buildings lined the streets. They stood solidly block by block.
Elaborate curlicues were chiseled into the façade under
each window frame, and above each one, in sharp sandstone
relief, the craftsmen placed miniature roofs. According to
the fancy of the architect the blank spaces in these roofs
were populated with gargoyle heads or lion manes, or fat little angels floating up toward the peak where they held
wreaths like halos as though ready to place them on the
inhabitants' curious heads as they poked out on a warm
summer day. The great entry doors of heavy oak had brass

handles, keyholes the size of Saint Peter's heavenly gate, and a design of concentric rectangles, rhomboids, or recessed rosettes. In a word, the neighborhood was solid. It conveyed safety and protection to all living in it.

But then came the bombs. The angels were powerless. In fact, they had their fat toes, hands and chunks of their behinds shaken loose by the violent reverberations. The great doors hung loose on their hinges. The sidewalks became littered with glass, or else gigantic heaps of brick and concrete settled over them and into the streets like chunky lava. A few trees stood like sad survivors mourning their fallen and buried brothers. And under all that rubble of concrete, brick, trees, power poles and wires, hidden like a treasure to be dug out, lay the silvery tracks of the Electric.

Otto and I explored the rubble heaps like treasure hunters. Not far, just seven heaps from our apartment, we had found the remnants of Hörlberg Park. Before the destruction, the streetcar tracks oddly ran through the park cutting it into halves. A fountain had graced one side, a playground sandbox and climbing apparatus the other. Now, a gaping crater had replaced the toddlers little paradise, and rubble from the surrounding buildings had partially buried the fountain. This was the place where I first met Inge. She had stood off to the side watching Otto and me, as we tossed bricks and rocks carelessly into the crater. She never said a word. When we showed up, she showed up. She wore a frayed sweater that hung lower than her hands. She appeared handless. Spindly legs protruded from a short black skirt. Her shoes were scuffed, her socks gray and sagging. She watched silently. She stood apart. Her lips were two tight lines and her forehead creased into a permanent frown over sea-blue eyes. She appeared defiant as well as aloof. Yet, her stance seemed defensive like a weary animal ready to join the feeding if asked, or to run off if confronted. Her dark brown hair stood out in bristles. Someone had tried to force it into two braids, Heidi-style.

Like shy mama's boys Otto and I feigned disinterest. After all, we—now in the long awaited years of early adolescence—pretended to have other business to attend to: climbing ruins, digging in heaps of rubble, throwing rocks, smashing glass in abandoned buildings. But soon Otto's eye began to twitch.

"I don't like being watched," he whispered in my ear, "you never know—"

The liar. He pretended war-time suspicions. Otto, know-it-all and expert on girls under hazelnut bushes, just twitched and grunted and said, "Let's scare her away."

Perhaps it was defiance toward the older Otto, perhaps it had been Mother speaking to me suddenly, but I said, "Nah, let her join—" I choked at my own surprise.

Otto shook his head violently. But scaring her had also been discarded.

"Widen your horizons," Mother had been hammering me lately. "Otto, it's always Otto. Only childish games. And almost fifteen! Look at his friends! Troublemakers his friends are." She was of course referring to Mueller, the knapsack fanatic who carried twisted bomb fragments around for sale as mementos, and Schuh (Schuhmeister) whose main interest in life was a Nazi dagger with which he showed his fearlessness by splaying the fingers of his left hand on a piece of wood and then stabbing the spaces between them as quickly as possible. But I was already on my way to independence, tentative though it was. I was plotting excuses to lure Otto to the park with me so I could get a glimpse of that girl. I could not possibly show up there by myself. I would have had to say something. But what?

Mother again, this time in an ugly twist, inadvertently helped me along. It was a mother's idea of weaning her son from his boyhood buddies and offering him alternatives.

Her idea crystallized in the form of a friend's daughter, Maria. She was a wonderful girl, she said, a good Vienna girl. It was time, that I at my age, as an adolescent, get acclimatized to other social situations including the opposite sex, like Maria—in whom, of course, I had no interest. She barely reached my shoulders, wore her hair in curled madness, walked with her toes pointed in, had a face full of freckles that glowed like pimples when she blushed, and worst of all, she bounced up and down at every step as though she were ready for a wild sprint up to the top of the Alps. In other words, the exact opposite of my girl in the park. My girl was mild as a doe, flawless as glass, a blue-eyed marvel, with a bee's waist, and a hand that would soon, I hoped, seek mine and then, after a while, more intimately, would love the warmth of my trouser pockets. I did not need, I did not want Maria, but Mother could not see past her plan in spite of my wildest and meanest protestations. The mad woman arranged for Maria to meet me at the apartment. "Here is some money. Go to the movies. Yes, yes. She is a nice girl," she implored. "Young people must get together. Go on. Don't be shy. Go on already." I went, pale with hate and pentup violence. I couldn't very well blow my cover. But by God I walked three feet apart from her with my nose in the air. I didn't utter a word. There. That would cure Mother, I thought.

I never saw Maria again. Guilt racked me. Mother tortured me with icy treatment. I fancied the episode made her hate me, made her invent abominable names for me, and made her contemplate murder. But I was free and Mother was forever cured as a coupling master.

The girl of *my* dreams lived in a third floor apartment abutting the Hörlberg Park. When she wasn't standing at fifty paces watching, she peered down from her window. I had never seen her play with anyone. Otto and I gently floated apart. Sure, we still played street soccer and went roaming with Shuh and Mueller. But more often than not I ran down to Hörlberg Park to see if I could lure her to the window just by standing below and using telepathy. I often did.

From a shy wave of the hand I advanced to a smile as a form of greeting, then I would casually lean against the new fencing that had been built around the park or sit nonchalantly on a pile of construction debris. I assumed an attitude of waiting for a bus. Of course there was no bus. The nearest bus route was several blocks away. "Hey," I silently called to my girl up there, "want to wait here with me?"

Soon, my aggressive self called loud and clear. "Wave her down," it urged. "She'll jump at the chance." But then my soft side panicked. "What then? What if she really comes down? What will I say? What will I do?" No answers came. A nasty frog grew in my throat. It grew and grew until it was an enormous lump too large to swallow.

Suddenly, a brilliant idea cooled my overzealous frog. Not far down the winding Schlackenheim Street that began around the corner from the park was the Schwarzenberg Kino. The cinema had recently reopened with preoccupation escape movies like *Woman of my Dreams, Vienna Blood*, and *Edelweiss Hunter*. I would invite her to go to the movie. I knew instinctively that a movie like that would be perfect. The details of how this perfection would play itself out I could not have formulated. Somehow I knew it would work. Just to get her to come down from her high perch, that was the crucial task.

"Hey," I called boldly from the tunnel formed by my hands around the mouth. "Want to come down?" I waved bravely.

She had stared for a moment. Then she had vanished. Then she had reappeared at the window. "I come already," she called back.

In three minutes she stepped from the doorway. It seemed so natural. She ran up to me. She smiled.

"What then?" she asked.

"We can—you and I—" There was the damned frog again. I swallowed hard. "Perhaps the Kino? Alright?"

"Sure," she said. "Where then?" She displayed so much confidence it floored me. Like nothing out of the ordinary had just taken place. I better match her cool attitude stride for stride, I told myself.

"Down there," I pointed toward the Schlackenheim Street. "The Schwarzenberg Kino. It's not far. I've been there hundreds of times."

"Inside?" she laughed. "You bragger!"

"Yes," I insisted, as we began walking. "My friend Otto and I have seen *Heartbeats* three times and only paid once."

She simply laughed and looked at me askance. I was glad she was enjoying herself. I could lie and brag forever if I had to. I'd keep her smiling like that all day.

"What's your name?" I asked. "Tell me yours and I tell you mine."

"Inge," she said. "And I know yours already. Willy—"

"You were eavesdropping." It was my turn to laugh.

I had no idea what the movie of the day was. All I knew was that showings were spaced two hours apart beginning at 2:30. We had plenty of time to make the 4:30. But what I wanted to show her was *our* way—Otto's and mine: how to sneak into the theater without paying, or how to see a forbidden movie—forbidden for children without a parent—by keeping hard on the heals of a woman, or a couple, pretending to belong to them.

Inge shrieked. "Not with me, no!"

"Oh, it's easy. Just follow me." There was my tone of superiority I had searched for. It seemed so easy when one was talking from the vantage point of real experience.

We were in luck. The movie was popular. A small crowd waited to be let in at the door. Men, women, a few kids. The movie was *The Berchtold Family*. The poster showed a passionate kiss against a backdrop of an estate with children running around and mysterious dark figures at the margins. Now if only Inge could hold down her giggles and concentrate on my every move.

I grabbed her hand and pulled her swiftly into the middle of the waiting group. Her hand felt warm and dry. I held on even though it was no longer necessary. Inge didn't pull away. I felt my heart surge. I was already victorious. Once inside the Kino, undiscovered, my status would rise to greater and greater heights in her eyes, I was sure.

We rushed in. We surged by the ticket attendant. Eyes forward. Confident strides. We found the darkest seats in the back. We were in.

I eagerly waited for the kissing scenes. I was fascinated by the slow probing approach of lips to lips, as though they were trying to taste each other before actually touching. The Berchtold girl was passively holding her lips toward Karl Heinz, the cavalry officer's son, who came forward so agonizingly slow that I wanted to shove him forward. Mach schnell, I wanted to yell out. Hurry up, you idiot. After all, she could faint and then where would he be? I felt strange sitting next to Inge during those scenes. There was a fear we were doing something terribly wrong, although we didn't do anything at all. Our hands had separated since we had sidled into our seats. But it was toward the end when Inge's hand looked for mine and we held on.

"Want to see it again?" I asked her.

"Again? Now?"

"We can hide behind that curtain there until the next showing begins."

"You are crazy, Willy," she laughed. "No, no. I must go

home. I'm sure you know that."

Inge and I went to the Kino again and again. We went to the Donaukanal. We strolled to the bridge that led to the Prater. But we couldn't go further. The Russians still occupied that part of the city. Although it was possible to get permits to cross over the demarcation line, it was said to be risky with the Russians.

On a warm day in August I kissed Inge. It was almost like Karl-Heinz and the Berchtold girl. They had been hiding in the family's "state" room, the Herrenzimmer, while the father was away. But Inge and I stood in the rough and tumble doorway at the edge of Hörlberg Park.

We had walked along the Donaukanal and threw stones into the sluggish water. Inge had been especially needy that day. She constantly wanted to walk so close that our arms and hips touched. I couldn't even walk a straight line. And all she wanted to talk about was the fact that we had been going out together for sooo many weeks. Wasn't it amazing? she asked. We were always walking so much, and Kino-going. It was close to a complaint. I didn't know why she acted like this. It sounded like she had suddenly decided that she no longer had any fun with it. Actually, it hadn't been weeks. Since the first Kino it had only been thirteen days. I was certain.

When we came to her door to say good-bye she came up to me so close I could smell her breath and I could see the lines and cracks in her lips that looked rough and soft at the same time. The upper one curved out and then in, the lower one had one smooth sweep. That was the one that was fatter.

"Do you want to kiss me?" she nearly whispered. "I'm a Vienna girl just like Helga Berchtold, don't you know?"

"A Vienna girl—" I said. My frog had suddenly awakened. All I could do was croak and cough and try to swallow it down. Meanwhile her lips were close, so close. Wasn't this what I had wanted? Had I not thought about this opportunity since the first Kino visit? What then, Willy, I said to myself, are you waiting for?

I kissed Inge. It was slow. But not so slow as in the movie. I would not want to be shoved from behind and then kind of fall on her. Her lips had tasted like nothing. It was the texture of the lips touching that made me remain there for a long time, and I found the early roughness dissipated into the softest sensation imaginable. It was like the melting of a pastry, like Vienna kisses. First the rough texture which then gave way to the smooth chocolate-nut-sugary-vanilla-coffee mixture as it broke up to be absorbed. And then the touch of the tip of the tongue, tongue to tongue, like the cool marmalade topping in the dimple of the Vienna kiss. We lasted a long time.

I ran home. I realized I had sweat streaking under my shirt. I had heated up like a 300 degree oven. It must have been the strain of standing muscle-bound in the same position for, I was sure, fifteen minutes.

"Inge," I said to the air around me. "Inge!" Was a God out there listening? I wanted to be thankful and plead for continuance. I believed Karl-Heinz had had the same thoughts when he said "Helga."

๛๛๛ Epilogue ๛๛๛

Do not Freeze. Eat Now.

They found Roland Gööck, the popular Viennese baker, smiling, but dead as a doornail in his office chair. The pen had slipped from his hand. The work was done. His life was done. His book manuscript was complete. The great reaper had graciously waited until the manuscript was finished, then walked right in past the large baking pans packed with pastries like soldier phalanxcs, through the clouds of sweet aroma, past the simmering ovens, and then he reaped. This man in the black cape, Mr. D., is not evil. He simply does what he is told. Thanks to his restraint, Roland Gööck's book was complete, and Roland was assured life after death in many a kitchen where baking was a labor of love. In Mr. D.'s Book of Life Roland had been marked "imminent." So what could he do? Roland had worked very hard, day after day, year after year. Up early, to bed late. He was an example of life's great ironies. He created pastries that made your heart warm, pastries that made you feel divine and thus they made you treat others divinely. Mr. D. had watched him work like a dog, watched him aggravate his heart condition. Of course he wouldn't interfere. It was not his purpose to interfere. He simply waited for the human on his list to do himself in. He would merely complete the journey the man had set upon long ago and then take him home. He stood and watched as Roland worked. The assistant bakers shook their flour-dusted heads. The master worked right alongside them all day long and then at the end of the day, when they went home to hearth and family, Roland stayed. Then he'd sit down in his office and work on his book. Finally, when he had finished the last of his recipes, Z for Zopf, and when he'd nailed down the final words, "the good flavor suffers," a farewell warning of what not to do, as though he were blowing a kiss to his audience out there, Roland Gööck took the hand Mr. D. offered.

I was just a kid fresh escaped from the war hanging on

to the skirt of my mother. But the name Gööck was an idea deeply embedded in the Vienna psyche since long before the war. The Gööck Bakery was a meeting place. When you were near the Graben Plaza it was natural to stop at Gööck's as though the aroma emanating from his shop pulled irresistibly. Your sweetheart dragged you there for a delicious pastry. But Gööck died at the end of the war and his shop closed. What remained was his manuscript. In due time the book was published by Meyer & Meyer, GmbH. Little did I know that I would meet him decades later, three thousand miles away. It contained everything mouth watering from Ananas fruit pie to Zopf. And under the "W" were, of course, the Wiener Küsse (Vienna Kisses).

I hurried out of the library. The traveled book lay on the passenger seat of my car. I glanced at it as I drove. Would it not be fun to make these Vienna Kisses come to life?

"Guess what I found at the library?" I called out from the door like a school boy waving a good report card.

"What then, Schatzi?" my wife called back from the kitchen.

I rushed up to her and hugged her—my wife of over thirty years, spindly still, as pretty as ever. Big eyes, ready to laugh, sensuous lips, ready to kiss. Had Otto and I proceeded to scare her back then in the Hörlberg Park. She might have passed away for good into the mist of time.

"Inge," I said breathlessly, "how about a Vienna Kiss?"

I was Karl-Heinz once again drifting toward those flavorful lips.

"Now?" she said alarmed, looking down at herself, at the apron around her waist and the rubber gloves on her hands.

Roland Gööck did not believe in freezing pastries. To freeze, then thaw, then freeze again, was as close to sin as a baker, amateur or professional, could commit. The last entry in his book closes in typical German with its lecture style and its structural convulsion:

"...once thawed deep frozen pastry work should not again frozen be. The good flavor suffers!"

Indeed, Vienna Kisses are to be consummated as soon as possible.